"You're both in danger."

Cade spoke the truth. Danger swirled around her. Jenna blew out a breath and sagged against the car.

He leaned in and kissed her on the mouth, short and oh-so-sweet. "We can get to the Prospero outpost by nightfall if we get moving. Lunch on the road."

Cade circled the car to the driver's side, and Jenna had to peel herself from the car door. That man's touch still worked magic. He posed a grave danger and had the ability to take something precious away from her.

Her heart.

CAROL
ERICSON

RUN, HIDE

♦ HARLEQUIN®INTRIGUE®

Recycling programs
for this product may
not exist in your area.

ISBN-13: 978-0-373-69676-5

RUN, HIDE   MAR 1 8 2014

Copyright © 2013 by Carol Ericson

Printed in U.S.A.

www.Harlequin.com

ABOUT THE AUTHOR

Carol Ericson lives with her husband and two sons in Southern California, home of state-of-the-art cosmetic surgery, wild freeway chases, palm trees bending in the Santa Ana winds and a million amazing stories. These stories, along with hordes of virile men and feisty women, clamor for release from Carol's head. It makes for some interesting headaches until she sets them free to fulfill their destinies and her readers' fantasies. To find out more about Carol, her books and her strange headaches, please visit her website, www.carolericson.com, "where romance flirts with danger."

Books by Carol Ericson

CAST OF CHARACTERS

Cade Stark—Prospero Team Three agent, he's on a mission to bring down an international arms dealer, but when that arms dealer goes after Cade's family, it gets personal. And now Cade must protect his wife and the son he barely knows from a threat he knows too well.

Jenna Stark—Cade's wife has been running and hiding ever since Cade's first assignment with Prospero garnered him a powerful enemy, but now Cade's back in her life and Jenna's determined to do anything to keep him there…even if it means confronting a threat bigger than the both of them.

Gavin Stark—The son Cade has seen only from afar, now a bargaining chip in a dangerous game of cat and mouse.

Beth Warren—A Prospero support agent, she risks her life to settle Cade and his family in a secure location, but does she know too much to be trusted?

Kevin Stark—Cade's father, whose rambling lifestyle has always gotten him in trouble, and he doesn't mind bringing others down with him—even his own family.

Horace Jimerson—He mans an outpost station in support of Prospero's intelligence effort, but maybe he's been "off the grid" for too long.

Nico Zendaris—An international arms dealer who was burned by Prospero Team Three; now he wants revenge and nothing's going to get in his way this time.

Chapter One

They'd found her son.

Jenna put her hand over the boy's mouth and held a finger to her lips. His dark eyes, wide above the rim of her hand, danced with excitement. He knew the game.

Only this time it was for real.

The heavy footsteps above them shook the floor. Jenna curled her body around Gavin's, like a mama bear hibernating with her cub. Protective. Fierce.

The muffled voices volleyed back and forth, punctuated by crashing furniture and banging closet doors. How many? Two? Three? She'd kill every last one of them to save Gavin from their clutches.

The throwaway cell phone in the pocket of her sweater buzzed and she clutched it in her fist, pushing a button with her thumb to turn it off. She could call 9-1-1, but she knew it was pointless. The people ransacking her house wouldn't let a small, local police department stop them. Worse, they might have already turned the police against her.

Better to hide.

Better to melt away.

Gavin squirmed in her arms, so she loosened her vise-like grip. He whimpered and she shushed him. Did he realize this exercise had gone beyond pretending?

He looked up at her with a pouty face and a trembling

lower lip. She cuddled him close and whispered in his ear. "Just a little bit longer."

Her eyes adjusted to the dark, and she gazed around the space beneath the slats of the wood flooring. The bundle of cash she stowed down here dug into her hip. She'd kept it for a rainy day, and it was pouring now.

With her arms wrapped around Gavin, her elbows almost touched the sides of the enclosure. They couldn't stay here long. When they first moved in here, she'd identified this spot as a place where she and Gavin could hide out from intruders...not take up temporary residence.

Another thump and a crash had Gavin clinging to her neck even more tightly. Despite the chill of the dank air, sweat dampened her armpits. She ran her tongue around her parched mouth.

Her muscles ached with the tension of keeping still and the weight of her son's body crushing against her. She stroked his hair with a shaky hand and murmured reassurances that she didn't feel.

A booted footstep stomped over her head, and she instinctively ducked. *Please don't look down. Please don't see the gap in the wood.*

She shivered as a low voice rumbled above them. She caught maybe every third word and couldn't make sense of the one-sided dialogue. So there were at least two of them.

Would they stay? Would they wait for her return?

Her car had been in the shop for the past week. She'd railed against the inconvenience, but now that broken fuel pump and the fact that her mechanic hadn't been able to get his hands on the right parts might've saved her life. Her car missing from the driveway may have given the men ransacking her house the impression that she wasn't home yet. Good.

Or would they sit and wait for her to drive up to the house? Not good.

Gavin snuffled and tapped her on the shoulder. Drawing back from him, she wedged a knuckle beneath his chin and tilted his head. She put two fingertips to his lips just in case he'd forgotten that they didn't speak when hiding in their secret place.

His mouth formed a stubborn line and he scrunched up his freckled nose. She knew that look…like father, like son. She couldn't keep Gavin in here forever—or even the next half hour.

She jerked her head to the side at the sound of a higher-pitched voice, a woman's voice, across the room by the front door. Could that be Marti?

Fear trickled down her back like a drip from an ice cube. *Oh, God, Marti, run. Get out of here.*

The low voices answered the high voice. If she could only hear the conversation.

The door slammed, and Gavin dug his grubby fingers into her shoulders, making a move to push against the wood slats that served as a door to their hideaway.

She clutched him tighter and shook her head and whispered, "Not yet."

Her limbs frozen, she cocked her head and listened. Was that a truck? The same truck that had sent her and Gavin scrambling for the floorboards fifteen minutes earlier?

She bit her lip so hard that she drew a salty drop of blood. Ten more minutes. They could wait ten more minutes if it meant the difference between life and death.

The hinges of the front door squeaked as someone pushed through again. Soft footsteps stole across the floor, and Jenna drew in a breath and held it.

The footsteps shuffled to the next room, the bedroom, and someone slid open the mirrored closet door. The intruder wandered into the second bedroom and the bathroom before returning to the living room.

The floor creaked to the right of Jenna's ear and she heard a voice. "Jenna? Are you here? It's okay. They're gone."

"Marti." Jenna sobbed with relief and knocked the heel of her hand against the floorboards. One slat shifted, weak daylight filtering through the space.

Marti gasped. "Are you under the floor?"

Jenna pushed against the second floorboard and blinked against the light that spilled onto her face. She gripped Gavin under the arms and hoisted him out first.

Marti's waiting arms pulled him up and against her chest. "Hey, buddy. Having some fun playing hide-and-seek?"

Shifting Gavin to her hip, Marti widened her eyes at Jenna clambering from the hiding place, clutching her purse against one side of her body and the bundle of cash against the other.

"Who were they, Jenna?"

"I'm not sure." Jenna dropped her purse and the stacks of money on a table. She brushed a few cobwebs from her arms and shook out her short hair. "What happened out here?"

"Isn't it obvious?" Marti swept her arm around the room at the upended tables and tossed cushions. "Those guys were looking for something."

"I mean, what happened with you? How did you get them out?"

"I saw the door ajar and heard noises, so I pushed open the door and asked them what the hell they were doing."

"You didn't!" Jenna clapped her hands over her mouth. "Were you trying to get yourself killed?"

"I had this baby." Marti dipped into the pocket of her

jacket and drew out a gun, just far enough for Jenna to see before shoving it back inside. "I brandished it and told them to get lost."

Jenna threw her arms around Marti and Gavin. "Just one more reason I'm glad you're my next-door neighbor." Her gaze darted to the window. "But they'll be back."

"Then let's call the cops. I told them that's what I was going to do."

"No!" Jenna held out her arms for Gavin and he slid from Marti's embrace to hers. She dragged in a shuddering breath and injected a cheery tone into her voice for Gavin's sake. "Do you want a cookie? You did such a great job with the game this time."

As Gavin nodded, Jenna carried him into the kitchen with Marti's eyeballs burning a hole in her back. She settled him on a chair at the kitchen table, rummaged through the cupboard and the fridge and placed a plate with two cookies and a glass of milk in front of him.

Marti came up behind Gavin and ruffled his hair. "What just happened, Jenna? Who were those guys?"

"I'm telling you the truth, Marti. I don't know."

"But you do know why you hid under the floorboards when they got here, and apparently it's not the first time you and Gavin have been under there."

Jenna dabbed at a lone chocolate chip from Gavin's plate and sucked it into her mouth, the sweetness replacing the metallic aftertaste of fear. "I told you never to ask me any questions, Marti. For your own safety."

"A-are you in some kind of witness protection program? That's what I always figured."

"Sort of." Her gaze wandered to the kitchen window, and a voice surfaced from her past.

If they ever find you, run.

"Can't the authorities who put you here help?" Marti was talking again, but Jenna was only half listening.

"We have to leave." She swept the cup and plate from the table and ran some water over them in the sink.

"Good idea." Marti tugged her down jacket around her. "Let's go to the police, and then maybe you can call the FBI or whoever put you in the program, and…"

Jenna grabbed Marti's arm. "No. I mean we have to leave—leave Lovett Peak for good."

Marti's mouth gaped open. "Like forever? Like now?"

Tears pricked the back of Jenna's eyes as she nodded. She'd miss Marti. She'd miss her adopted town of Lovett Peak, Utah. Just like all the other towns in all the other states.

"T-tell everyone I had a family emergency." She grabbed her bag from the table and shoved the bundle of money inside. Holding her hand out to her son, she said, "Let's go, honey bunny."

"You mean now?" Marti gripped her shoulders and shook her. "What about all your stuff? What about your life?"

Jenna took in the sparse little house with no photos, no mementos, nothing personal, and a smile twisted her lips. "There's not much stuff…not much life."

A fat tear rolled down Marti's cheek, smearing her makeup. "Can't you tell me what's happening, Jenna? Won't you let me help you?"

Jenna hugged her friend, her best friend for the past ten months she'd lived in Lovett Peak. "Thanks for everything, friend. And keep that gun handy for the next twenty-four hours.

"Let's go, Gavin."

"I'm going to miss you. Contact me when you can." Marti extended her arms for one last hug.

A crack split the air, and Marti froze. Her heavily lined eyes widened and her lipsticked mouth went slack. She toppled forward, the blood from the gaping wound in the back of her head spreading onto the battered linoleum floor.

Covering Gavin's face with one hand, Jenna screamed. The front window shattered and she ducked at the same time she realized the window had fallen apart from the bullet that had taken Marti's life.

Lifting her gaze to the snowy scene outside, she saw nothing—no gun, no gunman—but she knew they were out there somewhere.

Gavin whined and tried to peel her fingers from his face. "What's wrong with Marti?"

"She's sick, honey." Jenna crouched, covering Gavin with her body, and hustled him out the back door. If the assassins had their high-powered weapons aimed at the back of the house, too, she didn't stand a chance.

She jogged across her small backyard in a hunched-over position, her muscles tight, her breath coming out in short spurts visible in the frosty air. She waited for the next shot.

They'd aim for her. They wouldn't want to hit Gavin.

They just wanted to take him.

Shoving Gavin in front of her, Jenna swung through a gate that led to her neighbor's side yard…her other neighbor. The image of Marti slammed against her brain, and her gut rolled.

Focus. Transportation. With her car out of commission, she and Gavin had been taking the free shuttle buses around town. After a week, she had memorized their schedules.

Head down, she stumbled through her neighbor's yard, her boots slushing through the snow, half dragging, half carrying a complaining Gavin. Poking her head into the street, she set her sights on the Mountain View Hotel one block down.

The free shuttles made a stop at the hotel's side entrance to take the tourists to the ski resort and the downtown restaurants. Looking neither right nor left, Jenna scurried to the side of the hotel.

She flattened her body against the wall, clutching her purse with one hand and her son with the other. A couple of skiers gathered on the steps of the hotel, their skis and poles pointing skyward.

When the bus pulled to the curb, Jenna hunched behind the skiers. The doors cranked open and she lunged for the first step, sweeping Gavin along with her.

She nabbed a seat near the back door of the bus and slumped in it.

Gavin kicked his legs beside her. "Skiing?"

"Not today." She kept her voice low and hoped Gavin would do the same.

"Marti fell down."

A sob hitched in Jenna's throat. Those men had murdered Marti and it was all her fault. Her fault and *his*.

"Marti will be fine."

The bus lurched forward and trundled along the snow-plowed streets. Jenna raised her head high enough to peek out the window. Were they out there? Were they following her?

"Are you going to snowboard?"

Jenna's heart flipped and she grabbed the back of the seat in front of her.

A man had twisted around in his seat, his smile aimed at Gavin. Her son hunched his shoulders and darted a sideways glance at her. Then he shook his head.

The bus jerked to a stop, and the bus driver growled up front. "What the heck is going on now?"

Jenna's heart picked up speed and she bolted upright in her seat. She leaned into the aisle of the bus to see if she could look through the front windshield, but she couldn't see over the extended dashboard.

"What's wrong?

"Looks like a truck has stalled across the lane up ahead."

"A truck?" Jenna licked her dry lips. She'd seen a flash of a black truck out the window of her house, and that had been enough to send her scurrying for the crawl space beneath her living room floor. Her instincts had been right, then.

Were they right now?

Folding her body almost in half, she scooted up the aisle and peered out the front windshield.

"Miss, I'm going to have to ask you to take your seat."

The bus driver's voice sounded as if it was coming from a far distance as a spasm of fear twisted her gut.

The black truck loomed horizontally across the lane ahead and cars flowed around it on either side. The bus wouldn't be able to squeeze past the truck. They'd have to stop. Right in front of the truck. Would Marti's killers be brazen enough to snatch a boy from a public bus?

She'd bet on it, but not her life and not her son's life.

Jenna scrambled back to her seat and grabbed Gavin, tucking him under her arm.

"We have to get off. Now."

The bus driver eyed her in the rearview mirror. "Lady, we're in the middle of the street. You can get off when we stop ahead because there's no way we're getting around that truck."

Jenna kicked a booted foot against the back door of the bus, rattling its windows. "Let me out of here."

The other passengers turned wide eyes on Jenna, huffing and puffing by the door.

The more commotion the better.

She battered the door again with her other boot and screamed. "Open the door."

The doors squealed open and she stumbled down the steps. Looking both ways, she hopped into the street.

Gavin wailed. "I wanna snowboard."

She jogged to the sidewalk, glancing over her shoulder. Was the man by the truck looking her way?

What now? She hadn't gotten too far from her house... and Marti's dead body. She couldn't go back. She couldn't get her car—the mechanic just got the part this morning.

Think, Jenna.

She couldn't put any more lives in danger. She'd have to hop on another bus and get to the main bus depot in Salt Lake City. She had cash...lots of cash. She could get them two tickets to anywhere.

Hitching Gavin higher on her hip, she strode down the snow-dusted street in the opposite direction of the truck—like a woman with purpose. Like a woman with confidence and not in fear for her life.

She turned the next corner, her mind clicking through the streets of Lovett Peak, searching her memory bank for the nearest bus stop.

"Where are we going, Mommy?"

"Someplace warm, honey bunny."

Half a mile away, in front of the high school. That bus could get them to Salt Lake.

She'd start over. Build a new life. Again.

She straightened her spine and marched through the residential streets on her way to the local high school.

When the sound of a loud engine rumbled behind them, her heartbeat quickened along with her steps as she glanced over her shoulder at an older model blue car.

When the car slowed down, its engine growling like a predatory animal, she broke into a run.

She heard the door fly open and a man shouted. "Jenna, stop!"

She stumbled, nearly falling to her knees. She'd know that voice anywhere. It belonged to the man responsible for her life on the run.

Cade Stark.

Her husband.

Chapter Two

The emotions that galloped across Jenna's face in rapid succession—fear, shock, loathing—punched him in the gut.

But he had no time for explanations, no time for apologies. Two trained assassins lurked just blocks away.

"Get in the back, Jenna, and duck down."

She hesitated for a split second, glanced at Gavin's face, alert and curious, and started for the car.

Cade's gaze roamed hungrily over Gavin's small frame and regret crawled across his skin like a fungus. He had no time for remorse, either. Not now.

As soon as Jenna threw open the back door to the car, Cade ducked back into the vehicle. When the door slammed, he peeled away from the curb with a squeal and heard a thump of bodies against the seat.

Regret number two hundred and fifty-eight.

When he hit the intersection, he eased off the accelerator and stopped at the red light like a normal person. He looked in the rearview mirror, getting a glimpse of the top of Jenna's head, disheveled blond hair gleaming in the wintry sun.

His California beach girl living in the snow. Never thought he'd live to see the day. Never thought he'd live to see a lot of days.

"Scrunch down farther."

"Who's the man, Mommy?" Gavin's head popped up and Jenna tugged him down again.

"H-he's going to give us a ride, Gavin."

Cade gulped back the dull rage and sharp words. What did he expect? He'd take being his son's ride…for now.

Sirens blared amid the oncoming traffic and a cadre of emergency vehicles, lights flashing, turned the corner in front of him. Had the black truck caused more trouble on the street? Even the cops couldn't stop the men in that truck. Not the entire Lovett Peak P.D.

Gavin's head appeared in his rearview mirror again, bouncing up like a jack-in-the-box.

"Stay down, Gavin. You're not in your car seat, so you have to lie down, okay?" Jenna wrapped her arms around their squirrelly son and pulled him down.

Gavin's voice squeaked from the depths of the backseat. "Fire trucks!"

"I heard them. They're gone already."

Cade eyed his side mirror as the last of the emergency vehicles took another turn…toward Jenna's area of town.

Had they done something to Jenna's little house?

He scanned the sky behind him, looking for smoke or some other sign of mayhem from that side of town. Because when those types of men appeared, mayhem followed.

Of course, his track record wasn't much better than theirs.

Jenna asked in a muffled voice, "Where are we going?"

"Away."

"What are you doing here, Cade?"

"Long story."

She snorted and he could picture her rolling her baby blues. "When is it ever a short story?"

"Spy meets girl next door. Spy loses girl next door. Is

that short enough for you?" Before she could respond, he whistled through his teeth. "Hello."

"What?"

"There's a commotion up ahead."

"What kind of commotion?" Fear edged Jenna's voice, and Cade clutched the steering wheel, feeling her fear like a knife to the heart.

"Looks like a car's on fire." Narrowing his eyes, he pumped the brakes. This four-lane road, two lanes in each direction, was the only way in and out of Lovett Peak. Now every car leaving town had to crawl past the accident, squeezing into one lane. Coincidence?

"Is there a black truck involved?"

So she'd seen the truck. Damn. They'd gotten closer to her and Gavin than he'd expected.

"Not this time." He cranked the wheel and pulled out of the line of cars, making a sharp right turn onto a small mountain access road that led back to Lovett Peak Ski Resort.

"Oh, no." Jenna bolted upright in the seat. "We can't go back to town."

He tipped his head toward the main road. "We can't go out that way, either. Everyone going past that so-called accident is a sitting duck."

"And what will we be in Lovett Peak?"

"We'll be a family among other families."

She sucked in a noisy breath, but she didn't respond. Trying to let the irony sink in most likely.

"We'll blend in. Have some dinner. Talk."

"Is that safe?"

"I'll protect you." He'd been waiting three long years to say those words.

"We can't go to my house."

"Of course not. It's been compromised."

"It's been more than compromised." She sniffled and coughed. "A dead body's there."

Cade slammed on the brakes and lurched against his seat belt while the driver behind him leaned on his horn. "Gavin…"

"Conked out."

He blew out a breath. He didn't think Jenna would be bringing up a dead body in front of their son. "Who was it?"

"My neighbor Marti. She scared them off with her gun, but they returned…with a bigger gun."

Cade pounded the steering wheel. "They were in your house with a weapon?"

"We hid the first time they were there, but they came back. They didn't come in the house the second time. I think they were afraid the police would show up because Marti told them she'd called the cops."

"Did she?" The cops were never any use in these situations. He should know.

"I wouldn't let her." She sniffled again. "I wish I had."

"They shot her from outside?"

"They shot her with some kind of high-powered rifle with a silencer. The only thing I heard was the window shattering after the fact."

"My God, Jenna. And you got on the bus after that?"

She shot up in the backseat, her short, blond hair sticking up all over. "How do you know any of this? Why are you here?"

"Safety and food first." He studied her tousled blond hair in the rearview mirror. "And a long, brown wig for you."

"A wig?"

"You can make your transformation at the next gas station." He jerked his thumb over his shoulder. "I have a bag in the back with some…stuff, disguises."

"How did you…"

"Save it."

She opened her mouth to say something, rolled her eyes and flopped back onto the seat.

Cade knew the town of Lovett Peak, had studied maps and satellite pictures. Knew every mountain road, convenience store and pizza joint. But he still hadn't gotten here in time.

His hands convulsively clutched the steering wheel when he thought about how close the assassins had come to Jenna and Gavin. If they had been successful...

"Does anyone know you at Mike and Mo's Service Station?"

"No. Lovett Peak's not that small and I kept a low profile."

How could a gorgeous, sun-kissed blonde keep a low profile in a land of snow bunnies? But Jenna had lost her surfer-girl tan, chopped off her hair and bundled herself in parkas and snow boots.

Checking his mirror for the hundredth time, Cade swung into Mike and Mo's Service Station and parked around the back. No bathrooms on the outside meant bathrooms on the inside, and he didn't want to wake up Gavin or send his mother inside on her own to make a quick change.

He popped the trunk. "I'll get the stuff and you can change in the backseat."

"Just what am I changing?"

"Jacket for sure—that powder blue color is unmistakable—and your hair." Prettiest color he'd ever seen, like a field of waving wheat on a summer day.

He slid from the seat, dragging his gun from the passenger seat next to him and shoving it into the back of his waistband. He hoisted a black bag from the trunk and opened the back door.

He swallowed hard. Jenna had her feet on the floor, but

her body was tipped over on the seat with Gavin tucked against her. Gavin had grown so much…and he'd missed it all. He'd caught glimpses of his son now and then and had photos, but he hadn't been this close to him since his birth.

He stuffed the bag onto the floor next to Jenna's boots. "There's a black parka in there and a wig and some brown contact lenses—nonprescription."

Jenna eased into a sitting position and twisted her head back and forth, taking in the empty alley behind the gas station. "This is weird. Why do you have this stuff?"

"For an occasion like this." He crouched down and pawed through the bag. "I don't have any clothes for Gavin, but I do have this."

Jenna's eyes widened at the electric trimmer in his hand. "He doesn't need a shave."

Cade cracked a smile. "It's for his hair. Give him a buzz cut."

"Oh." Jenna ran her fingers through Gavin's brown, curly locks. "And what about you?"

He lifted a shoulder. "They don't know what I look like."

Sitting sideways in his seat with his gun in his lap, Cade kept one eye on the parking lot in front of them and one eye on Jenna in the backseat, shrugging off her blue jacket and stuffing her arms into the black one.

She slicked back her hair and tugged the wig over her head. A cascade of brown waves fell over her shoulders as she flipped her head back.

"Contacts?"

"In the side pocket."

She hunched over the bag and then leaned between the front seats to look in the rearview mirror.

Cade adjusted it for her and she scooted in closer, the scent of her light floral perfume stealing over him and tak-

ing him back to summer nights in San Diego and the bou-
gainvillea that crept up the trellis on her patio.

She caught his eye in the mirror. "Better?"

He nodded at the brown-eyed stranger.

Digging through her purse, she said, "Might as well have
the makeup match the coloring."

Whatever that meant.

Again, she leaned forward, this time the long hair of
the wig brushing the shoulder of his jacket. She pinched
a small brush between two fingers and stroked it over her
eyebrows, darkening them to match the hair. Next came
black mascara, applied liberally over her long lashes. She
blinked and then swiped a tube of lipstick across her lush
lips, turning her mouth into a dark pink pout.

Cade cocked his head. Maybe she should've gone mousy
instead of glam.

"What?" She was studying him in the mirror, a pink
blush heightening her color—a *natural* pink blush.

"It's just...I don't know." He ran a hand through his own
short hair. "You look incredible. You're going to attract a
lot of attention."

"But I don't look like Jenna James."

"No, you don't look like Jenna James, the single mom
and waitress at the Lovett Brewing Company." That Jenna
James would have to disappear.

She flattened her lips into a straight line. Hadn't she realized he'd been keeping tabs on her and Gavin these past
three years? Probably thought he'd forgotten all about them.

He didn't blame her.

"Are you done?" He held up the clippers. "Do you want
to do the honors, or do you want me to do it?"

"We can't cut off all his hair while he's sleeping." She
brushed Gavin's curls from his forehead. "That's a viola-
tion of his trust."

What did he know about raising kids?

"Can you wake him up?"

She continued stroking Gavin's face. "Wake up, sleepy-head."

Gavin murmured and rubbed a fist under his nose, and Jenna squeezed his shoulder. "Wake up, Gavin."

He blinked his eyes and popped up. He clapped both hands over his mouth and giggled. "Mommy?"

She tickled his cheek with the ends of her long hair. "Do you like it?"

"You look funny."

"Thank you." She thrust her hand, palm up, over Cade's shoulder. "Do you want to look funny, too?"

"Uh-huh." He bounced in his seat.

Cade slapped the electric hair clippers into her hand and she showed it to Gavin. "Do you want a haircut?"

Gavin pointed into the front seat. "Like him?"

Jenna's gaze flicked to Cade, her newly brown eyes narrowed. "Yeah, sort of like him."

Gavin nodded.

She pushed open the back door away from the entrance to the parking lot. "Scoot over here, so your hair will fall outside."

She flicked on the switch of the clippers, which vibrated in her hand, and ten minutes later, Gavin ran his hand over his buzz cut, grinning from ear to ear.

"I wanna see."

She scooped him onto her lap so he could see in the rearview mirror. Gavin giggled again, and a smile tugged at Cade's lips.

"Okay, now that you both look funny, let's go to Lovett Peak Ski Resort and get something to eat."

"Isn't that kind of...public?"

"Exactly." He started the car and snapped on his seat

belt. "It won't be easy for them to…uh…snatch their cargo in the middle of a ski resort, even if it does occur to them to look there."

Jenna's creamy skin paled even more, and Cade mentally gave himself a good, swift kick. If she didn't realize those guys were after Gavin, she did now. But maybe she needed to know.

Cade pulled the car into the parking lot of the ski resort, maneuvering around skiers and snowboarders packing it in for the day. He parked the car and waited while Jenna zipped up Gavin's jacket and pulled his mittens onto his hands.

When Jenna had Gavin properly bundled, Cade slipped his weapon in the inside pocket of his jacket and got out of the car. He opened Jenna's door and stood toe-to-toe with her for the first time since he'd blasted back into her life.

"You look good, Jenna."

"Yeah, because I just caked on about two inches of makeup."

He caught a long strand of the wig as it fluttered outside her hood and wrapped it around his finger. "I meant even before the disguise."

"Oh, you mean when I was tearing down the street with my son tucked under my arm after just witnessing…" She trailed off, glancing down at Gavin crushed against her side.

"I mean…" She had no intention of making this easy on him. He disengaged his finger and yanked the hood off her head. "You're a brunette. Let the casual observer see that."

They crunched across the parking lot as a light snow began to fall. More skiers and snowboarders headed to their cars or the city and hotel shuttle buses, the boarders clomping along in their heavy boots.

Gavin pointed a mittened hand at one of them. "Snow-board."

Cade's hand hovered above Gavin's head. He wanted to pick up his son, but would he allow that? Would his mother? "Have you been on a snowboard yet, Gavin?"

"No." He skipped once and slipped on the slushy snow at the edge of the parking lot.

To save Gavin from a fall, Cade scooped him up in his arms and buried his face in his neck. He didn't smell like a baby anymore. He smelled sticky and a little grungy. Just like a boy should.

Gavin laughed and kicked his legs. "Tickles."

Cade released a pent-up breath. At least his son hadn't pushed him away. "I'm ticklish, too."

He met Jenna's eyes over Gavin's head. *Ouch.* Did her blue eyes have as much fire as this brown pair? Or had he just forgotten?

Never. He remembered every minute detail of Jenna's face...and body.

"Uh, I'll just carry him to the lodge, if that's okay."

"It's okay with me." She shrugged. "And Gavin is friendly. He'll go with anyone."

Double ouch.

They climbed the stairs to the cafeteria situated in the resort's ski lodge. As Cade suspected, the après-ski crowd filled the restaurant, bodies, equipment and winter clothing taking up every spare inch of the place. He saw a few empty tables, but he didn't want to split up from Jenna while someone grabbed a table and someone else grabbed the food.

"What sounds good?"

Jenna tipped her chin at the counter for Italian food. "Gavin likes pizza and there should be some pasta there, too."

"Italian, it is." Cade continued to hold Gavin so he could

point out what kind of pizza he wanted, while he and Jenna decided on some pastas and sauces.

Jenna carried one tray with Gavin clinging to the pocket of her black jacket, and Cade gripped the other tray while negotiating the tables scattered around the cafeteria.

He zeroed in on a table by the fireplace where a set of parents and two kids were gathering their jackets and gloves. "Are you leaving?"

The dad handed a plastic tray to his son. "Yeah. Crazy in here, huh?"

"Crazy." Cade nodded. He pulled out a plastic chair for Jenna with one hand as he set the tray down with the other. Gavin crawled into the chair next to his mom's.

After several minutes of settling in, Jenna went for the throat. "So why are those people after us and what are you doing here?"

"Nothing like getting right to the point." His gaze flicked to Gavin, picking slices of pepperoni off his pizza and lining them up on his plate.

"I've been with you for almost an hour, and I still don't have answers—not that I expect many."

"I can't give you the details, Jenna. Just know you and Gavin have been on my radar ever since…"

"Ever since you left us."

He hunched over the table and whispered, "You know I didn't have a choice."

"I guess that's my fault. Should've never run off to Vegas with a drunken SEAL."

Cade's pasta slid down his throat the wrong way and he choked. He chugged half his bottle of water to wash it down. "I was *not* drunk. I knew exactly what I was doing."

Her lip trembled and she dabbed at a strand of cheese hanging from Gavin's chin. "That makes it worse. You knew you could never have a wife…a family, and you went ahead and married me, anyway."

"I didn't realize the full extent of the danger. When Jack Coburn recruited me…"

She smacked the table and the salt-and-pepper shakers jumped. "If I hear Jack Coburn's name one more time, I'm gonna puke."

Gavin had jerked when Jenna hit the table, but now a big smile split his pizza-stained face and he giggled. "Mommy's gonna puke."

This time Cade snorted water out of his nose. Eating with these two was hazardous to his health…almost as hazardous as his job was to theirs.

Smiling, Jenna swiped a napkin across Gavin's face. "Not really, silly."

She wiped the smile off her face just as quickly. "Why now, Cade? Did they step up their efforts to find us or did they just get lucky? Is there a fresh, new reason why we're back in their sights, or have we always been there?"

"It's not safe to tell you, Jenna."

"You mean it could actually get worse than living on the run, looking over my shoulder, being separated from… my family?"

Her words stung, but in a way she'd been right. It *was* all his fault. If he hadn't met her in Coronado, if he hadn't fallen for her harder than he'd ever fallen for any woman before, if he hadn't wanted to make her his wife, she'd be living a normal, happy life with some other guy. A safe guy.

She sighed and tossed her napkin onto her plate. "If you're not going to come clean, let's blow this joint."

"Okay, I suppose we should stop and get Gavin a car seat before we head to our next destination, right?"

"Next destination? And where would that be?"

"Someplace safe."

"We can't get a car seat at this time. Any store here that would have them is too far away and probably closed."

"I guess we'll have to keep him hidden."

She shoved back her plastic chair so hard that it almost hit the floor. "Wouldn't be the first time."

They dumped their trash in the can and stacked their trays on top. Nobody gave them a second look—a typical family on a ski vacation.

The light flakes of snow had dissipated, and the night sky had cleared to a deep midnight-blue so sharp it looked as if it could shatter into a million pieces.

Jenna opened the back door and tucked Gavin into the corner of the seat, snapping a seat belt around his waist. "Just this once you go without a car seat because we don't have one and it's too late to buy one."

Gavin yawned and nodded.

Jenna hung on the car door. "Am I sitting up front this time?"

"Not a great idea just yet. Why don't you snuggle up with Gavin in the back? I have a couple of blankets in the trunk."

She gave an exaggerated sigh, but he didn't believe for a minute she would be all that comfortable riding out of town shotgun.

He gathered one of the blankets from the trunk and tossed it onto her lap.

Cranking on the engine and the heater, he adjusted his rearview mirror. He hoped he hadn't made a mistake hanging around town.

He turned back onto the one highway in and out of Lovett Peak and the car rolled smoothly over the newly plowed asphalt. Traffic began to back up, and he slowed down, trying to peer ahead at the commotion.

When he curved around the next bend, he swore under his breath.

"What's wrong?"

"It's a police stop."

"What does that mean, a police stop?"

"The police are stopping cars, Jenna." He swiveled his head around to the right, but no escape magically appeared. A solid barrier between his lane and the oncoming traffic put an end to any ideas of a wide U-turn in the middle of the highway. The cops would be all over some car trying to avoid the stop.

"D-do you think it's a drunk-driving stop?"

"Could be." Cade slid his gun from his inside pocket and stored it beneath his seat. "Is Gavin sleeping?"

"Yes."

"You need to cover him and yourself with that blanket. If you can get down on the floor of the car, that's better."

The rustling in the backseat told him Jenna had complied with no fuss. Then it hit him. She was accustomed to looking over her shoulder. Thanks to him.

She asked in a muffled voice, "What are they doing?"

"Shh. Waving most people through. I think we're okay. No more talking."

Despite the snowdrifts on the side of the road, a trickle of sweat rolled down Cade's spine. One cop per lane ducked toward every window, said a few words and waved the driver through. He was up in two more cars.

He blew out a breath and rolled back his shoulders. He stretched his lips wide to practice a smile.

Rolling to a stop, he buzzed down his window. "What's going on, Officer?"

"We're looking for a woman with a child."

Cade peeled his tongue from the roof of his dry mouth. "Missing persons?"

"Ah, persons of interest." The cop flashed his light into the car, and Cade tensed his muscles.

"Did you do some skiing?"

"No. Just visited a friend." Cade loosened his clammy grip on the steering wheel.

The beam of light intruded into the backseat and Cade held his breath.

"Sir, what's under the blanket on the floor?"

"I have a blanket on the floor?"

"You do, sir, and I'm going to have to ask you to show me what's underneath."

Cade's calf ached as it hovered over the accelerator.

"No problem."

He reached for the keys as if preparing to shut off the ignition. Instead, he jammed his foot down on the gas pedal, and his car, with its 450-horsepower engine, lunged forward with a squeal and a roar.

Chapter Three

Jenna clutched Gavin to her body as the car seemed to leap from the road. Any second she expected bullets to shatter the back window.

"What's going on? Are they coming after us?"

"Keep down."

The car took a curve and it felt as if it were balancing on two wheels. "My God, what kind of car is this, the Bat Mobile?"

"Close. It's designed to outrun any cop car in the nation."

"And is it fulfilling its promise?"

"Just about."

Jenna strained her ears but couldn't detect the sound of a siren over the roar of the car's engine. "Are they after us?"

"Sort of."

"Why would they be looking for me?"

"You sure ask a lot of questions. I'm in the middle of a car chase here."

"Should've asked a few more questions in Vegas."

"We got this. Although they'll probably call ahead for backup, so we're going to have to ditch the car."

"Now?"

"Not right this minute. Don't worry."

"Don't worry? You're kidding, right?"

The car turned off the highway, and Jenna lifted a corner

of the blanket. The lights of the highway had disappeared and the car skimmed through the darkness.

"Where are we going, Cade?"

"An abandoned warehouse. The car will fit and no one will be the wiser, especially those cops I just left in my dust."

"We're spending the night in an abandoned warehouse?" She threw off the blanket and pulled Gavin back onto the seat. How he'd slept through the Bat Mobile's flight over a barely paved road, she had no idea.

"Would you rather be in a jail cell with no protection?"

She would've scoffed at the notion that she had no protection in a cell at the police station, but she knew Cade's foes better than that. They'd probably been the ones who'd notified the police to look out for a woman and child in connection with Marti's murder.

She peeked out the window at the black night. The stars sparkled in the clear sky, but the sliver of moon cast only a stingy glow on the snow.

The stealth car cruised down the unplowed road, its back end fishtailing here and there when it hit a patch of ice it couldn't handle.

A hulking shape loomed ahead, and Jenna shivered instinctively. It wasn't exactly the Hotel del Coronado, where she and Cade had spent one glorious, sun-washed weekend.

The car jerked to a stop and Cade rocketed from the front seat, clutching his gun in one hand and a set of keys in the other.

He unlocked the front door of the warehouse and rolled it open as it squealed in protest. He slid back into the car and eased it through the gaping entrance. Then he made a U-turn and parked the car facing the doorway. Ready for blast-off.

Jenna scooted out of the car and hugged her new jacket

around her body. "Why did you happen to have a key to an abandoned warehouse on the outskirts of Lovett Peak?"

"Don't ask."

"Oops, I forgot." She hunched her shoulders. "It's freezing in here."

"I'll get the heat going in the car, and I have a second blanket in the trunk along with some water and snacks."

"Is being a spy sort of like being a Boy Scout? You're always prepared?"

"Something like that." A grin split his impossibly handsome face, a face she'd never been able to vanquish from her mind. "I'm glad to see you haven't lost your sense of humor."

"You think I'm joking?" She shook her head, but the truth had slapped her in the face like a snowball. She hadn't felt this alive in three years. Even before Cade had been recruited for Prospero, his crooked smile and flashing dark eyes had spelled danger and she'd fallen hook, line and sinker.

Her wealthy parents had spoiled her, with stuff not attention, and she'd spent her childhood and teenage years acting out, trying to get them to react. They never did.

But she wasn't a spoiled, flighty girl anymore. She had Gavin, and she couldn't afford to live dangerously…or any more dangerously than she'd already been living.

Cade crouched by the open door and tucked the blanket around Gavin. "I can't believe he slept through that."

"He's accustomed to upset and upheaval." A second later she felt a stab of regret at her words and tone, as Cade's face, full of wonder over his son, darkened and creased.

"It's no way for a kid to live. He needs stability and Little League games and a best friend."

"Are you going to tell me why we're in danger now? *More* danger? You owe me that much, Cade."

Cade squeezed his eyes closed and pinched the bridge of his nose, looking older than his twenty-nine years. "They think I have something, Jenna, but I don't."

She squeezed past him and sat on the backseat, her legs dangling out of the car. "Who are *they,* Cade?"

He shrugged as if the *they* didn't matter. "An arms dealer named Nico Zendaris—the same man who put a target on my back after my first mission with Prospero. A band of engineers from nations hostile to the United States got together and developed something that's very bad news for us. Zendaris laid claim to the plans for the weapon's prototype and now those plans are missing. Zendaris thinks I have them."

"What are the plans for?"

"I've told you too much already."

She'd get that out of him later. "Why does this arms dealer think you have the plans?"

"Because I did have them."

She pressed her hands against her bouncing knees. "What happened to them?"

"Someone stole them."

"And he doesn't believe you?"

"Not a chance."

"He will when the person who stole them makes a move. The thief stole them for a reason—money, power, influence. He's going to tip his hand soon."

"But right now it's better for that person to let everyone believe I still have those plans."

"And now Zendaris knows about Gavin."

"That's right."

"He's leverage, isn't he? I'm fairly dispensable, but if they get their hands on your son, they have you right where they want you."

"I wouldn't call you dispensable, Jenna." He brushed

her cheek with his knuckle and she shivered for a different reason than the chill in the warehouse. "Unfortunately, I can't give them what they want."

She snorted. "You wouldn't even if you could."

"I'd do anything for Gavin." He tweaked the blanket around his son's legs. "I gave him up to keep him safe."

"You wouldn't give up your job for the same reason."

Cade clenched his jaw and the easygoing man she'd fallen in love with in San Diego morphed into the tough-as-nails Navy SEAL she'd caught rare glimpses of once they'd gotten married.

Had she pushed him too far?

He shoved away from the car and the cold air rushed in. Despite what her mind screamed, her body craved the warmth of his touch, his nearness, his protection. Because she was tired of doing it all on her own.

The car bounced as Cade opened the trunk. He strode back to the gaping door and dropped a blanket into her lap. "You two huddle up back here. I'll run the car intermittently. Don't want to die of carbon monoxide poisoning in an abandoned warehouse."

And just like that, the precariousness of their situation stabbed Jenna right through the heart.

"What about you?"

"I'm good up front." He slammed her door and crawled into the driver's seat. Thrusting the second blanket between the two front seats, she said, "You can have this. Gavin and I can share, and we have body heat to warm us up."

Cade's dark eyes glittered, sending butterflies to her belly and warmth to her cheeks. Just mentioning body heat had them both thinking about the warm summer days in Coronado when they'd made love on the beach, in their private hot tub and in an intentionally stalled elevator.

"Keep it." He turned on the lights over the rearview

mirror, placed his weapon on the console and dragged a crumpled magazine from beneath the front passenger seat.

Okay, maybe *she* was the only one thinking about those warm summer days.

Sighing, she pushed her new brown hair out of her face and curled up next to Gavin, pulling the extra blanket over both of them. She'd never get to sleep with her husband flipping pages of a magazine two feet away from her.

She shifted Gavin's head onto her chest and dabbed at a line of drool on his cheek. Yanking the blanket over her shoulder, she rested her chin on top of Gavin's bristly hair and closed her eyes.

She couldn't sleep but drifted into a land of daydreams where she, her husband and her son lived in a small house with a white picket fence and a dog stationed in the front yard. A smile played across her lips as she indulged in the impossible scenario.

Just as she began to think she might actually doze off, sedated by happy, if unlikely, dreams, a loud thwacking noise had her bolting to an upright position.

"What the hell is that?"

Cade tossed his magazine to the floor of the car and grabbed his gun from the console. He aimed the barrel at the roof of the car and grimaced.

"It's a helicopter...and we've got company."

Chapter Four

"Grab Gavin." Cade tilted his head back and forth, following the sound of the helicopter as it swooped toward the roof of the warehouse and then began descending for a touchdown.

Had they given up their search by car and brought in the big guns? Unfortunately, this patch of land had just enough room to put down a chopper.

Jenna had scrambled from the car, clutching a bundled Gavin to her chest. "There are a bunch of barrels over in the corner."

"Is Gavin awake?"

"He's getting there."

"Is he going to be able to keep quiet if someone comes in here?"

"He's an old hand at hiding."

She couldn't resist twisting the knife, could she? And he felt every serrated edge.

"You're right. Those barrels are the best location because they're near the entrance."

He scrunched up Jenna's blue jacket underneath the blanket in the back to make it look as if someone was beneath it. He dragged his bag and backpack from the trunk. Then he locked all the doors. Might as well make them work to get in, providing a distraction.

Jenna had stopped short of the barrels. Couldn't she hear the blades of the helicopter slowing down? They were minutes away from game time.

"Let's move."

She pointed to a plastic jug nestled between the barrels. "Gasoline?"

Cade strode past her and with the toe of his boot nudged the jug. Liquid sloshed against the side. Leaning over, he twisted off the plastic lid on the spout. He sniffed the contents. "It *is* gasoline."

"W-we can use it to our advantage."

"Especially with the lighter I have in the glove compartment." He strode to the car to retrieve it, grateful that Coburn and Prospero had taught him well to prepare for anything.

Jenna's years on the run with Gavin had taught her well, too. And although Cade appreciated having a partner instead of a liability, her transformation caused guilt to flood his senses again. She'd been a pampered princess when he'd met her, with rows and rows of expensive shoes and designer dresses. Now she was on the road with not even an extra pair of underwear to her name.

As Cade returned to the barrels, Gavin stirred in Jenna's arms and yawned. Cade didn't want his son anywhere near this dangerous situation, but right now he didn't have a choice.

Pressing his hand between Jenna's shoulder blades, Cade said, "Duck behind the last barrel in the corner. I'll be right in front of you."

He crouched behind one of the barrels and pulled the gasoline container toward his feet. He withdrew his weapon from his waistband just as someone tried the handle on the warehouse door. A thump and a zipping noise told him someone had shot through the lock with a silencer.

Were they hoping to take Cade and Jenna by surprise? Hoping they hadn't heard the chopper's approach?

Gavin coughed and mumbled some words, and Jenna whispered an answer.

Cade clenched his muscles in readiness and against another wave of guilt. He couldn't afford to be sidetracked right now by emotion. As Jack Coburn had taught him and all the Prospero team members, you had to allow instinct to take over in life-or-death situations.

And this was life or death—his and his family's.

The doors to the warehouse creaked despite the stop-and-go approach used by the intruders. Light from the waiting helicopter crawled across the warehouse floor as the door widened.

"It's the car." The voice, slightly accented, had Cade gripping his gun even tighter.

Cade couldn't see the entrance to the warehouse and didn't dare make a move, but from the footsteps creeping across the floor, he could tell two people had entered the warehouse. The same two from the truck?

"Lots of places to hide in here." Another voice, this one with a Midwest twang. Zendaris had recruited far and wide for his henchmen.

"Then you'd better keep a lookout. They probably heard the helicopter."

"They? She has someone helping her, doesn't she? Do you think it's him?"

"I think you need to shut up and keep watch while I check out the car."

A figure outfitted in black from head to toe, his gun leading the way, moved into Cade's line of vision. Cade curled his fingers around the handle of the plastic jug, the thumb of his other hand rubbing against the grooved wheel of the lighter.

The man sidled against the car, disappearing from Cade's view. Then he hissed, "Someone's in there."

The lookout took a few steps toward the car, and Cade nudged Jenna in the side and pointed toward the warehouse door with the lighter.

On her knees clutching Gavin to her chest, she hobbled behind the next barrel.

A muscle in Cade's jaw twitched. He had to time this just right. The second man took one more step toward the car, and that's all Cade needed. He flicked the lighter once and held the dancing flame to the edge of a handkerchief he'd dragged from his pocket.

He turned his head toward Jenna and dipped his chin to his chest. Then he swung his arm, tossing his home-made Molotov cocktail toward the nondescript car with the souped-up engine.

Shouts echoed in the warehouse. With his bags strapped across his body, Cade hunched forward, running behind Jenna and Gavin, blocking them from anything that might hurtle from the belly of the warehouse.

The makeshift bomb exploded behind them, and the heat of it scorched Cade's back. He took a quick glance over his shoulder to make sure the wall of fire had created a barrier between them and Zendaris's men. Then he launched out the doorway, shoving Jenna in front of him.

"Keep moving. There might be another explosion if the fire reaches the car."

Gavin started yelling, fully awake now. His inarticulate cries washed over Cade, but Cade didn't have time to process them. Didn't have time to feel guilty. Not now.

Jenna headed toward the unpaved road, the brown hair of her wig flying behind her.

Cade caught her arm. "Where are you going?"

She turned, and the flames from the warehouse shimmered in her eyes. "Away from here."

"I've got a faster way." He jerked his thumb over his shoulder at the helicopter perched in a clearing beside the warehouse.

"Are you kidding?" She stumbled back, and he scooped Gavin from her arms.

"Nope. Hop inside the passenger seat. I know this type of chopper and there are a couple of seats in the back where we can secure Gavin."

Looking into his son's frightened face, he touched his nose. "Do you want to ride in a helicopter?"

Gavin nodded, but then cranked his head to the side, his eyes widening as they took in the blazing warehouse.

Gunshots pierced through the roar from the fire. "They might be trying to get out the back way. Hurry."

Jenna scrambled for the chopper, and Cade ducked inside to settle Gavin on a jump seat in the back, tossing his bags in the other seat. "Buckle his seat belt, Jenna, while I get this bird in the air."

Cade dropped onto the seat and started flicking switches. He'd had helicopter flight experience during both his SEAL and Prospero trainings. Zendaris's cohorts couldn't have chosen a better getaway vehicle.

Jenna slammed into her own seat and pulled the seat belt over her head. She grabbed a pair of headphones and held them up. Cade nodded, and she slipped them on over the wig.

The engine sputtered and the blades started cranking. Cade thrust the throttle forward and the chopper lifted from the dirt.

Jenna tugged on his sleeve and pointed to the ground. Two figures were stumbling from the back of the warehouse, which was belching black smoke. In unison, the pale circle of their faces turned toward the sky. One of the men raised his weapon.

Jenna screamed and reached into the back, as if she could protect Gavin from a bullet with her bare hands.

Cade shouted. "It's okay, they can't reach us. They probably can't even see straight."

The chopper continued its climb, swooping and bobbing, leaving behind the glowing warehouse, the puffs of black smoke and two angry men.

Cade took a deep breath and stabilized the helicopter. He buzzed over the snow-covered ground, avoiding the highway. He had to get Jenna and Gavin away from here. Where? He didn't know yet.

He checked the fuel gauge. At least they had enough fuel to get them out of this area.

Jenna tapped him on the arm and shouted, but the noise drowned out her words.

He pointed to his own headphones and pulled the microphone down, positioning it in front of his mouth. She did the same, and Cade reached over and pressed a button on her headpiece.

He spoke into his mic. "Can you hear me?"

She shouted back, "Yes!" and he jumped in his seat.

"You don't need to yell anymore." He tapped his headphone on the right side. "I can hear you just fine. Are you okay?"

"Perfect, Cade. I'm riding in a helicopter over snow-covered mountains to God knows where with my son stashed in the back like a piece of luggage. Perfect."

"Could be worse."

"Yeah, it could always be worse."

He squeezed her knee. "I meant are you okay physically? No smoke inhalation? No burns?"

"I'm fine." She reached back and pulled the blanket around Gavin. "Where are we going?"

"Our options changed with the acquisition of this chopper." He snapped his fingers. "There's a place not too far from here but just far enough where we can regroup."

"Does it happen to have a landing pad?"

"Not exactly, but I'll be able to put this baby down nearby. How's Gavin holding up?"

"He's wide-awake and staring out the window."

"We'll have him wrapped up and snug in front of a fire before too long."

"We just left a fire. That one didn't work out too well."

Cade clenched his teeth. Would she ever forgive him for abandoning her and Gavin?

Would he ever forgive himself?

SOONER THAN JENNA EXPECTED, Cade began bringing the chopper down for a landing. Her neck ached from twisting her head around every few minutes to check on Gavin. He'd caught on pretty quickly that she couldn't hear him above the noise in the helicopter, and had contented himself with leaning his forehead against the fiberglass window and staring at the darkened landscape whizzing below them.

Even though Cade could hear her through his headphones, she'd kept mostly silent. Her grandmother always told her if you didn't have anything nice to say, keep your mouth shut.

Cade's smooth voice flowed through her headphones once again. "I'm putting her down right here. We should be safe, for now."

He just had to add the *for now.* Not that she hadn't figured that out for herself. Sometimes she felt as if she and Gavin would be on the run forever. Until she died.

She pressed her nose against the fiberglass. The dark

splotch on the ground must be a clearing. Cade knew what he was doing. Cade always knew what he was doing—except for the night he married her.

The helicopter descended in a vertical line and touched down like a feather landing on the grass.

Cade flipped some switches, adjusted some knobs and the thwacking sound of the blades slowed to a hiss.

Jenna peered out the window at trees on all sides and marveled at Cade's skill in landing this contraption. How had he known precisely where to put it?

Then another question crowded out her admiration for Cade. Where the heck were they?

Before she could give voice to her concerns, Cade hopped out of the helicopter and circled to her side. He pulled open the door. "Everyone doing okay?"

"That was fun!" Gavin bounced up and down in his seat.

An ear-to-ear grin split Cade's face. "Glad you enjoyed the ride. Now we're going to get some sleep."

Jenna jabbed a finger toward the trees. "In there?"

"There's a cabin nearby." He snapped open her seat belt. "It's about half a mile. I'll carry Gavin and my bag if you get the backpack."

Tugging her jacket around her body, Jenna scooted toward the door. Cade held out his hand and she took it as he helped her to the ground. Then he reached into the back of the chopper and freed Gavin from his seat belt.

Cade hoisted his black bag over his head, strapping it diagonally across his body. He slipped the straps of the backpack over Jenna's shoulders. She staggered back under its weight.

Cade steadied her. "Sorry. I've got my life in there right now." Then he lifted Gavin from his seat and clasped him to his body once outside.

"Are you ready for a short hike?"

"What's a short hike after what we've been through to-night?"

"Can we take the helicopter?" Gavin wriggled in Cade's arms.

Too much excitement had flooded his little body with adrenaline. *Welcome to life with Dad, kiddo.*

"Too many trees, Gavin. Choppers need wide, open spaces." Cade pulled a flashlight from his pocket and aimed it at the ground. "I'll lead the way. Stick close."

Stick close? Three years of abandonment, and now she was supposed to stick close?

She grunted a response and lined up behind Cade as he made his way through the trees, following some obscure trail only he could see. She stumbled a few times and bumped her forehead against his back once, but they didn't stop.

After about fifteen minutes of heavy breathing and scuffing through pine needles, the trees abruptly ended. Jenna glanced up from the ground to catch sight of a small log cabin nestled against a boulder of about the same size. Despite its darkened windows and cold chimney, the cabin exuded a cozy vibe.

"What is this place?"

"It's a Prospero safe house."

"Prospero and safe house in the same breath is an oxymoron."

Cade hoisted Gavin in his arms and lifted one brow in her direction. "Then you don't know much about Prospero."

"I know more than I want to know."

Cade blew out a breath, which puffed away in the cold air.

"Are we still in Utah?"

"Yeah, but farther south than Salt Lake."

"Do you have a key to this place, too, or do you just mumble the secret Prospero code?"

"You're funny, Jenna, always were…in a sarcastic kind of way."

"Yeah, I've been a barrel of laughs the past three years."

He chucked her under the chin. "You couldn't have been jumping at your shadow all that time or you never could've raised a confident boy like this one."

Pleasure crept across her skin at the compliment, but she shook it off. He always did know how to butter her up.

Cade swung Gavin to the ground. "You and your mom wait at the front door, okay?"

Gavin scampered toward the cabin and hopped up the two steps.

"Where are you going?" Jenna grabbed the slick sleeve of his down jacket.

"No secret Prospero code. I have to break a window in the back. I'll open the door for you and Gavin."

"Sh-should I have a gun or something?" She rubbed the arms of her own jacket, as her gaze darted around the perimeter of the cabin.

"Nobody knows where this place is…yet."

He'd used that word again. She guessed he didn't want to inspire a false sense of security.

She joined Gavin on the wooden porch and leaned against the post that ran to the roof. Someone had been maintaining this place, which meant someone else knew of its location.

The dead bolt on the inside of the door snapped, and Jenna jumped.

Cade poked his head outside. "Welcome to my humble abode."

"Any abode is better than sleeping in a car in a cold warehouse."

"Exactly." He swung open the door. "So thoughtful of our pursuers to loan us their helicopter."

Jenna scooped up Gavin beneath his arms and swung him over the threshold.

Cade snapped the door shut behind them and hunched forward to click on a lamp. The yellow glow spilled across the floor.

"Electricity?"

"Electricity and water. I can't vouch for what's in the fridge, but there should be some imperishable snacks in the kitchen and there's a stack of wood on the hearth."

Jenna gave an involuntary shiver. The cold had seeped so far into her bones that she'd forgotten it had taken up residence until Cade had mentioned the hearth. The thought of a warm fire, a friendly fire, caused her skin to tingle.

"So, first things first." Cade crouched by the fireplace and began crumpling newspapers from the stack in the corner. He glanced at one of the headlines. "Four months ago. I wonder who used it last?"

"I'm just glad whoever it was didn't gobble up all the wood." She settled Gavin in a chair facing the fireplace. "You stay here while your...Cade and I get this thing started."

She'd have to break it to Gavin at some point that the man whizzing them around in fast cars and helicopters was his father. Then what? Introduce him to a father just in time for that father to disappear?

She scrunched a newspaper in her fists and shoved it beneath the grate. "Is this enough?"

"I think that'll do." Cade dragged a split of wood from a brass holder on the hearth and tossed it onto the grate. He stacked three more on top of that one, and touched the flame from his lighter to the paper beneath them.

The ends of the newspaper curled and large, pillowing ashes drifted up the chimney.

"Mommy."

Jenna turned to find Gavin positioned at the edge of the chair, his eyes wide, reflecting the burgeoning fire.

She walked on her knees toward him, arms held out. When she reached her son, she engulfed him in a hug. "This fire's okay. It's in a fireplace and it's going to stay right there."

He squiggled out of her grasp and peered around her shoulder at the blaze crackling to life.

Reaching around her, Cade grabbed the legs of Gavin's chair and scooted it forward. "Take your boots off and warm your toes."

Cade collapsed on the floor, dug his elbow into the area rug and rested his chin in the palm of his hand. "Feels good, huh?"

Gavin kicked his legs. "Shoes, Mommy."

"You got it." She untied Gavin's boots and pulled them off his feet. She stripped off his slightly damp socks and chafed his toes between her palms. "Better?"

He nodded and snuggled against the back of the chair.

Jenna wrapped the blanket around him, but he shoved his legs forward, his toes curling in the warmth of the fire.

She pressed her back against the bottom of the chair, crossed one leg over the other and untied her own boots.

Cade hopped up from the floor. "I think there are some blankets in the closet."

Did he expect her to cuddle up with him in front of a roaring fire? She tossed aside her second boot. She wanted nothing more at this moment.

Gavin's outstretched legs drooped, his feet skimming Jenna's shoulder. Turning, she pulled the blanket over his legs. He shifted to the side and curled his legs beneath him, resting his head on the arm of the overstuffed chair.

Cade returned and shook out another blanket, which he laid over Gavin. "Electricity's on, water's on, but not the gas, so the only heat we have in here is this fire. He'll be warmer sleeping in the chair than in one of the cold bedrooms back there."

Her cheeks warm, Jenna busied herself with tucking the loose ends of the blanket around Gavin's body. And where would she and Cade be warmer sleeping?

He pulled another chair close to the fireplace and dropped to the floor in front of it, wrapping a blanket around his shoulders. He shoved another blanket toward her with his foot. "There are a couple more blankets on the beds, if you're still cold."

Folding her legs on the thin area rug, she dragged the blanket toward her. "Maybe another one on top of this rug."

"Yeah, too bad it's not one of those bearskin rugs."

He pushed to his feet again, the blanket hanging from his frame like a serape. He returned a minute later with a patchwork bedspread. "I'll cover the rug with this."

Jenna scrambled to her feet and took the other end of the bedspread from Cade. They spread it out on the floor, and Jenna sank down on the fluffy softness, parking her back against Gavin's chair again.

Cade propped himself against the other chair, stretching his long legs toward the fire. He'd removed his boots and his bare feet poked out of the end of the blanket.

"Are you sure you don't want to remove your jacket? It's warm enough now without it, and yours has to be as wet as mine was."

She didn't want to remove any more clothing than necessary, but he had a point. Her damp jacket felt soggy next to the warm, dry blanket.

She shrugged off the blanket and unzipped her jacket. She spread it out on the floor to the side of the fireplace. Then she tugged the wig off her head and ran her hands through her short hair. "How long are we safe here?"

Cade tapped the side of his eye. "Do you want to remove the contacts, too? You probably don't want to sleep in them and I think you can dispense with the disguise."

Jenna reached up and pulled down her bottom lid while running her index finger over her eyeball to remove the lens. She repeated with the second eye and flicked both brown contacts onto the table next to Gavin's chair.

Did Cade suggest that to distract her from her question? He had the wrong fugitive. "How long are we safe?"

"With that helicopter parked a half mile away?" He snorted. "Not long. They may even have a tracking device on it."

"Long enough to get some sleep?"

"Absolutely. It's going to take them some time to round up more transportation, especially another helicopter." He dragged a gun from beneath the chair. "You plan to sleep sitting upright like that?"

"Do you?"

"I could sleep hanging from my thumbs with one eye open."

"You're not going to sleep, are you?"

"Sure I am—with one eye open."

No point in arguing with the man. She knew better. Hadn't she tried to talk him out of that whirlwind marriage four years ago?

Puffing her cheeks and blowing out a breath, she scooted away from her backrest, clutching the blanket around her body with one hand. She tipped over onto the floor, curling her legs to her chest, her back to Cade.

"Comfortable?"

"Uh-huh." How could she possibly be comfortable with her long-lost, sex appeal–oozing, magnetic husband breathing down her back?

He rustled beside her and she tightened her fetal position. Her eyes flew open when a soft pillow hit the back of her head.

"Sorry about that." He plucked the round pillow from the floor and dangled it over her face. "You might be more comfortable with this wedged under your head."

"Thanks." She snatched the pillow from him and scrunched it beneath her cheek. "Much better. Wake me up when the bullets start flying."

For the second time that night, Jenna drifted off with Cade just inches away from her. She tugged the blanket toward her chin, a smile curving her lips. This was easier than she'd expected.

Her husband didn't have the same impact on her as before.

She unfurled her legs and straightened her back. Her limbs felt heavy and her eyelids heavier as she succumbed to heavenly sleep.

THE LAST WISPS OF A PLEASANT dream floated out of her grasp, and she sighed. She snuggled into the warm, comfortable pillow and it shifted beneath her.

Fluttering her lashes, she smoothed her hand across the pillow, which had somehow made it beneath her blanket during the night.

The pillow shifted again.

She blinked her eyes and rolled to her back. She gulped and tension seized every one of her muscles, dragging her out of her drowsy comfort.

She wasn't staring down the barrel of a gun, but this was worse. Much worse.

She was staring into the dark eyes of Cade Stark, her head was in his lap and it felt oh, so good.

Chapter Five

Uh-oh.

Jenna had looked beautiful in her sleep, her short, blond hair framing her face, her lashes creating two crescents on her milky skin. Burrowing into his lap.

She looked no less beautiful now with her blue eyes snapping to attention and a rose-colored flush marching across her cheeks. But he knew he was seconds away from losing her.

Her head shot up. "How did I get over here?"

Would she believe him if he told her she'd inched her way toward him during the night as she'd slept? Of course, he'd helped the situation along when the top of her head met the outside of his thigh by placing her head on his lap.

"You sort of rolled over here." He held up his hands. "You're still fully clothed."

Her jaw tightened.

Wrong moment to try humor. It had always worked with her before, usually defusing any tension between them. But this level of tension was a whole new ball game. They'd stumbled into unchartered areas of tension, and he had no idea how to make it better.

Cuddling her while she slept had made it worse. For her.

He'd enjoyed every second of it.

She scooted toward Gavin, still snoozing in the arms of the big chair. "No problems last night?"

Other than having his beautiful wife's head lolling against his thighs all night and not being able to make a move?

"No problems." He tapped the cell phone in the breast pocket of his shirt. "Can't get any service, though."

She smoothed her hand across Gavin's forehead. "And if you could?"

"I'd call one of my contacts for transportation out of here. We can't fly around in a helicopter."

"You can just call Prospero on a regular cell phone? What's the number? 1-800-SPY-4YOU?"

"You're a laugh a minute." He plucked the phone from his pocket and cradled it in his palm. "This baby is no ordinary cell phone."

"Of course not."

"It's untraceable. No numbers are stored on it. You can't do things like call back."

"But you're still limited by pedestrian stuff like no service."

"True." He dropped the useless phone back in his pocket.

She yawned and stretched, then dropped her hand back to Gavin's forehead, stroking his skin. "We can't take the helicopter out for another spin?"

"The bird doesn't have much gas left."

Her hand stilled and trembled. "You mean we're stuck here?"

"We have our legs." He slapped his thigh. "Are you hungry?"

"Is there anything to eat in there?" She tipped her chin toward the kitchen.

"Nothing much. Don't know if I'd trust any food out of that kitchen, anyway." He hunched forward and dragged his bag toward him. "I have a few snacks in here—energy bars, beef jerky, bottled water."

"You lead a strange existence." She folded her arms and hunched her shoulders. "Where have you been all these years?"

"Three years, Jenna." He buried his head in the duffel and plucked out a couple of energy bars. He tossed one to her. "I've been overseas mostly, but I've been back and forth to the States."

"Guess I missed your postcards." She tore open the energy bar and ripped off a piece with her teeth.

He dragged in a breath. "I checked up on you, you and Gavin."

Blinking her eyes, she swallowed. "How did you manage that?"

"I had Prospero keep tabs on you here. Whenever I could, I staked out your location...just to see you and Gavin for myself."

She stuffed another piece of energy bar in her mouth and said, "That's kind of creepy."

His gaze shifted to his son, sleeping in the chair with his hand curled beneath his chubby cheek. "Not creepy at all."

"Is that how you knew we were in Lovett Peak?"

"Yeah." He hoisted himself up and perched on the arm of Gavin's makeshift bed. "Do you think he'll eat an energy bar for breakfast?"

She ignored his question, hell-bent on a few of her own.

"Did you know those men were coming after me and Gavin?"

"I figured they might try to find you again."

"Again?" She narrowed her eyes. "Had they given up? Was I running for no good reason after your mission went south?"

"I wouldn't say that."

"So they renewed their efforts after their first attempts, when they thought you'd stolen those plans or whatever they are."

"Those plans are very important to Zendaris. He's willing to do anything to get them back."

She studied him across the sleeping form of their son. "How did you lose them? I take it we wouldn't be in this predicament if you'd been able to turn them over to the government, correct? There's nothing Zendaris could've done at that point. Game over."

"Probably, but I didn't have the plans in my possession for very long before they were snatched from me."

"Did someone steal them out of the backseat of your car, or what? You always used to throw junk in the back of your car and forget about it for weeks."

A smile tugged at his mouth despite their *predicament*, as she'd called it. "Not exactly. The plans were in a file on my computer. I wasn't going to use regular email to get them to the CIA. But before I could encrypt them or get one of our computer guys on it, someone hacked into my computer and lifted them."

"No trace left behind?"

"None." He jumped up from the chair and paced to the window, running a hand through his hair. "Whoever stole those plans knew his way around a computer. We had our cyber-threat guys go through my PC, and they couldn't detect anything."

She yanked Gavin's blanket over his shoulder and smoothed imaginary creases from it. "Maybe all we have to do is keep out of sight until whoever has those plans makes Zendaris an offer he can't refuse."

"It's not that simple."

"Where you're concerned, it never is."

This time he ignored her. "The person who stole the

plans may not want to make a deal with Zendaris at all. Maybe he wants to replace Zendaris as top-dog arms dealer and sell the plans to the highest bidding terrorist organization or rogue nation."

"Then Zendaris will find out soon enough." She spread her arms to encompass the small room. "Isn't there some sort of terrorist network where that kind of news would travel fast?"

"There is and it does."

"So, again, once Zendaris realizes you don't have the plans, he'll back off. We...Gavin and I will be safe."

"Never did like the idea of relying on something out of my control to keep my family safe. I don't want to sit around and wait for the person with the plans to make his move."

"What does that mean?"

"Prospero is planning to go after Zendaris."

"Why haven't you before?"

Cade propped up the mantel with his shoulder. "He's evasive, slippery. We don't even know what Zendaris looks like. We don't know where he lives. We don't know if he has a family."

"Wow, Prospero is really slipping." She tossed her head, and her gleaming hair caught the weak light seeping into the room from the east-facing window. "I guess Jack Coburn isn't superhuman, after all."

Case shook his head and chuckled. "He'd be shocked to hear himself described as superhuman."

"That's how you made him come across. You idolized him."

Jenna's blue eyes fogged over with wistfulness. As ridiculous as it seemed, Cade knew Jenna had always felt he'd chosen Jack Coburn over her when he'd decided to join Prospero.

Well, hadn't he? Just like his father had chosen the life of a con man over staying with his family. Cade had learned how to abandon his family at the knee of a master.

He shrugged off the mantel and circled behind Gavin's chair. He leaned his forearms on the back, hunching over his son. "Coburn's a good man, Jenna, an honorable man, but I didn't join Prospero out of any blind hero-worship."

"I guess I don't blame you for joining Prospero so much as I blame you for marrying me when you knew darn well the life of a secret agent loomed in your future."

He leaned farther over the chair, nearly touching her forehead with his. "That was totally your fault. One look at you, and I could no more resist you than I could turn down any cockamamy dare."

She drew back. "Don't change the subject. Do you have any idea who might have taken the plans from you?"

"Could be any number of people or groups, but whoever has them would want to keep his identity secret for as long as possible to keep Zendaris off his tail."

"And keep him on ours."

"Exactly."

"Once you catch Zendaris, Gavin and I can stop running."

"Once we catch Zendaris…" How many times had he repeated those words to himself? They'd taken on an almost-magical quality because they represented freedom for him, freedom to claim his family.

His gaze shifted to Jenna, watching as she ran her hand across Gavin's new buzz cut. Would he be able to claim them? Would Jenna take him back?

He had to make sure she'd want nothing more.

"Yes? Once you catch Zendaris?"

Was she holding her breath or was he?

He cleared his throat. "You and Gavin will be safe once Zendaris is out of the picture."

"I'm sure Prospero has plenty of enemies. How can I be sure there won't be another one ready to take Zendaris's place, ready to threaten me and my son?"

Our son.

"There's only one Zendaris. With him, it's personal."

"You never did explain what happened on your first assignment with Prospero. All I know is you left me and then returned only to warn me to get lost and never show my face again."

He braced his forehead against his clasped hands. "I know it must've seemed that way, but I warned you out of necessity. After we completed our mission, Zendaris found out about our families and vowed to take revenge."

"That must've been one heckuva mission. What did you do to him?"

"We spoiled his biggest arms deal to date." Cade closed his eyes as heat surged through his body, even the memories powerful enough to pump adrenaline into his veins.

"What did he expect, and how is that personal? These guys have to know everything isn't going to come up roses for them all the time. He's still in business, isn't he?"

Cade glanced at Jenna, wrinkling her nose. "What do you mean?"

"I mean for Zendaris to want to come after you personally, you must've hit him on more than a business level."

"Funny you should mention that." Cade crossed in front of Jenna to grab his blanket rumpled on the floor. "We, my Prospero teammates and I, thought the same thing."

"Were any of Zendaris's people injured or killed during your mission?"

"A few."

"Any women or children?"

Cade clenched his jaw. "We don't attack women and children. That's his M.O."

"Okay, okay." She held up her hands. "Family members, maybe?"

"Could be. We're not sure." He folded his blanket and reached for Jenna's. "I told you, we don't know much about him. Don't know what he looks like. Don't know anything about his family."

"You knew enough to prevent that first deal from going down."

"Good intelligence all around on that job, but we'd like nothing more than to nail the guy...in person. End his career."

She sighed. "Sounds good to me, too."

Gavin stirred and fluttered his eyelashes. He opened one eye, sleepy at first and then widening as he took in his surroundings. He bolted upright.

"Shh." Jenna scooted into the chair beside him, nudging him with her hip. "It's okay. Do you remember coming to this place last night?"

"In the helicopter." He pointed a finger at Cade. "With him."

"That's Cade. He's going to be with us for...a while. A little while."

If he had anything to say about it, he'd be with them a lot longer than that. He'd left shortly after Gavin was born, so he had a lot of smiles to make up for.

Cade dug another energy bar from his pocket and waved it at Jenna. "Will he eat this?"

"Candy bar!" Gavin bounced in the chair, aiming a hopeful look at his mother.

"Not really." She took the bar from Cade and ripped one silver-foiled corner. "Do you want to try it?"

Licking his lips, Gavin nodded.

Cade now regretted not getting the chocolate-covered ones. The kid was in for a rude surprise.

Jenna broke off a piece and held it out to Gavin. He pinched it between two small fingers and shoved it into his mouth.

Wrinkling his nose, he stuck out his tongue, half-chewed bits of energy bar clinging to it.

"Gavin, do not spit that out."

"It's not a candy bar. I want eggs."

Cade sucked in a breath and cupped his hand beneath Gavin's chin. "You can spit it in my hand."

Gavin didn't need an engraved invitation for that. He spat the little ball of goo into Cade's palm, while Jenna's brows disappeared beneath her blond bangs.

"Uh, let me get rid of this, and then we'll find some eggs."

When he returned to the living room after dumping the glob of food into the trash and washing his hands, Jenna had folded the rest of the blankets and was holding a bottle of water to Gavin's mouth as he drank.

"Where are we going to get eggs?"

"A diner."

"Where are we going to find a diner with a helicopter pad? Oh, yeah, no helicopter. How are we going to reach a diner on foot, with lugging bags and a kid?"

He dangled a keychain from his finger. "Where there's a Prospero safe house, there's usually a Prospero safe car."

"There's a car parked out here somewhere?" She dabbed Gavin's dribbling chin with the hem of her fleece shirt."

He swung the keys around his finger. "I found these hanging on a hook in the kitchen. There's definitely a car key on this ring."

"Where's the car?"

"There's a road on the other side of that bunch of trees. It's probably parked there. A car couldn't get through the trees."

"What about the helicopter?"

"I have to get rid of it."

"How do you get rid of a helicopter?"

"Blow it up."

She clucked her tongue. "You Prospero agents are nothing more than a bunch of adolescent brains in men's bodies—high speed chases, blowing things up, disguises."

"Yeah, it would almost be fun if it weren't deadly serious."

"Believe me, I know how deadly serious it is." She combed her fingers through her gleaming strands. "Do you think I have time to take a shower before we blow up anything?"

"Sure. I hope you don't mind if I skip mine."

She paused, digging her nails into her scalp. "Because we're still in danger."

His eyes darted toward Gavin. "Yeah."

"Then I'll skip it, too. Let's blow this joint...not literally. Don't get any ideas."

"Will you and Gavin be okay here while I check the shed? I'm going to look for tools, materials or anything else we can use."

"If you can't find anything, how do you plan to blow up the helicopter?"

He shrugged. "It still has some gas in the tank. One well-placed bullet and kaboom."

"Gavin and I will come with you."

"Good idea."

Cade shoved the keychain in the front pocket of his jeans and pulled on his parka.

Jenna zipped up Gavin in his jacket and stuffed his hands into his mittens. "We're going outside. Stay right beside me."

Cade's gun, concealed in the pocket of his parka, bumped

his thigh as he crossed the room and opened the front door of the cabin. No snow had moved in overnight, and the crisp, cold morning nipped at his cheeks.

He glanced both ways before stepping onto the porch. The serene scene mocked their circumstances. This cabin could be the perfect setting for a cozy family getaway…or a romantic interlude.

But the stillness didn't fool him. That chopper sitting less than a mile away represented a huge target. He had to get rid of it.

He stomped across the frozen ground with Jenna and Gavin keeping pace beside him. Jenna had a firm grip on Gavin's hand, even though his head was swiveling in twenty different directions, trying to take in his surroundings.

He liked that his boy carried an air of adventure and mischief about him. Jenna had done a good job not turning him into a scared, little rabbit, even though she'd had every reason to do so.

They reached the door of the shed, secured with a dull silver padlock. Cade dragged the keys from his pocket and selected a small one from the key ring. "I think this one should do it."

"You Prospero boys think of everything, don't you?"

Hooking his finger around the padlock and lifting it, he said over his shoulder, "It's a good organization, Jenna. We do good work, important work. And we get zero recognition for it. Sometimes the work we do is even denied by our own government."

"I know that, Cade." She put her gloved hand on the slick sleeve of his jacket. "I just wish it hadn't been you called to this duty."

His gaze locked with hers. The heat crackled between them despite the frosty air. He wanted her back in his life, and he planned to pull out all the stops to get her there even if he had to go into hiding with her and Gavin until Prospero brought down Zendaris.

Zendaris had ripped Cade's wife and son away from him. If Zendaris hadn't made it his mission in life to discover the identities of the agents involved in that raid, and then followed up by targeting their families, Cade could've been with Jenna these past three years. He could've been there for his son.

Other agents had families. Hell, even Jack Coburn had a family.

He brushed a wisp of hair from Jenna's red cheek. "I'll make it up to you. I swear."

Her eyes filled with tears, and Cade didn't know if it was the emotion between them or just the cold air. Whatever the reason, she ducked to scoop up Gavin's mitten, which had fallen to the ground.

Cade turned to the shed. Tugging at the lock, he inserted the key and yanked it free. The wooden door swung open. The shed didn't have electricity, but the doorway and a window on the back wall afforded enough light to illuminate the small space.

Cade shuffled inside with Jenna and Gavin close behind him. Shelves lined the walls with all manner of tools and supplies filling every inch of them. "I'm surprised nobody has discovered this place yet and ransacked it."

"Must be the giant *P* on the door indicating Prospero property."

"I never get tired of your humor, Jenna."

Gavin zipped between them, arms outstretched, making a beeline toward one of the shelves.

"Whoa." Cade grabbed the hood of Gavin's jacket and he bounced backward into Cade's legs. "Oops. Sorry about that, but you can't go running around in here."

"You don't have to yank him around like he's a terrorist. He's three." Jenna stepped between them and brushed off Gavin's jacket like she was brushing off Cade's cooties.

"Really?" Cade ran his knuckles across Gavin's head. "Because I thought he was sixteen."

Gavin giggled and held up three fingers. "Three!"

Cade cocked his head. "Must be the haircut."

Jenna pursed her lips against the smile wobbling there. "He broke away from me. I guess all this stuff—" she waved her arms around the interior of the shed "—looks irresistible."

"Looks irresistible to me, too." He let his gaze caress her soft, tousled hair and her face, rosy from the chill in the air.

She jerked her head toward the junk on the shelves. "Do you think you'll find what you need here to get rid of that chopper?"

"I think I should be able to rig something together."

"Then we find the car that you're so sure is located somewhere around here?"

"Prospero's safe houses are all outfitted the same—out-of-the-way places or plunked down in the middle of a busy city block, water, electricity, a change of clothing, weapons and some means of transportation."

He jingled the keys in his hand. "I know there's a car in our future."

Jenna opened her mouth, probably to respond with another sarcastic comment about Prospero, but a loud bang had them all jumping in place.

"That can't be good."

Cade scrambled for the door and peered over the tree line at a column of black smoke. All of his senses switched into the on position. "Looks like we won't have to blow up that chopper, after all."

"Y-you mean?"

"Someone beat us to it."

Chapter Six

Jenna crushed Gavin against her thigh, and he squirmed. "How did they find us so fast?"

Cade unzipped his duffel and began shoving items from the shelves into it. "Probably had a GPS on it. Even so, I'm surprised they got here so fast unless they used other people."

His nonchalance lit a fuse in her belly, and she stomped her foot. "What now? How are we going to get out of here?"

He looked up from his bag, dark brows raised. "I told you. We're driving out of here, and we'll have over a half-mile head start on them."

"There *might* be a car. There's no guarantee."

"With Prospero, there's always a guarantee."

"Yeah, always a guarantee that Prospero will ruin my life."

"You left your purse in the house with all that cash in it." He had the nerve to shove her from behind. "Go get it. Then we'll head out."

Clutching Gavin's hand, she made for the door.

"Leave Gavin here. You run in and out." He kicked the door wider. "I'll keep an eye on you."

Her gaze scanned the wooded scene beyond, like something out of Currier and Ives but with terrorists coming over the river and through the woods instead of some happy family. "How do we know they're not watching us right now?"

"They just blew up the helicopter. They're not ninja warriors. They can't get here in a nanosecond."

"Ninja warriors." Gavin repeated Cade's words, obviously fascinated with the idea of ninja warriors.

"Okay, but if anything happens, you take Gavin and run."

"Something will happen if you keep standing here jabbering. Move."

She spun around and dashed across clearing to the cabin. She stumbled up the steps and grabbed her purse from the back of the chair, pausing for a moment to take in the cozy room with the fire dying in the grate.

This place could've meant so much more for her and Cade if this had been a normal reunion. But nothing about her husband was normal. Nothing about her life was normal.

Her sniff turned into a snort and she slammed the door on normal and jogged back to her life.

Cade swung his bulging bag over his shoulder, secured his backpack once more over Jenna's shoulders and picked up Gavin, who kicked his feet against Cade's hip. "I know you're a big guy and would rather walk, but just at the beginning we need to hurry so I'm going to carry you for a while."

Cade had a smile on his face, but something in his tone brooked no argument, and Gavin recognized the voice of authority, the whine dying in his throat.

"How fast do you think they're coming?" Jenna squinted into the trees, her eyeballs aching.

"This house is not exactly on a well-worn path from the chopper. Do you remember all the roots and bushes we had to navigate to get here? They have four different directions to choose from. It doesn't mean they're going to pick the right one."

"And what about us? We have three different directions to choose from."

"Nope. I saw a map in the cabin. I know the direction of the road…and that car."

Hoisting Gavin onto his back, Cade strode toward a thicket of trees that looked impenetrable.

Jenna hugged her purse to her chest, folding her arms across it. "Do you want me to take the bag while you carry Gavin?"

"The bag is heavier than Gavin and you already have the backpack. I'm good. You just keep up."

Having Cade here to lead the way and make decisions had taken a weight from her shoulders, but it came with a price. She hadn't taken orders from anyone in a long time, and it left a bitter taste on her tongue.

She swallowed it. Now was not the time for petty one-upmanship. Cade could keep Gavin safe, and she had to hold on to that and shove her resentment aside.

They zigzagged through the trees, clambering over fallen trunks and dodging patches of ice. Jenna's breath came out in short spurts, fogging in front of her. Her stomach rumbled and she tripped over the next tree trunk and fell to her knees.

Cade turned and nearly stumbled over her. "Are you okay?"

"I'm fine."

He bent forward with Gavin clinging to his neck, and hooked his arms beneath hers. He righted and steadied her and for a second she wished she was the one in his arms.

She straightened her spine. "Thanks. Let's go."

"We should be at the road soon. You're probably starving. I know I am." He tugged at one of Gavin's legs dangling against his side. "How about you? Still want those eggs?"

"Yes, eggs."

"Okay, hang on."

Cade's legs started pumping again, like pistons, even, steady, strong. Did the man ever show weakness?

He hunched forward and pulled back the low branch of a tree. "There's the road."

"Is the car there?"

"Should be along here somewhere."

"Maybe someone took it already."

"We're going to walk along the side of the road, keeping close to the foliage in case we have to jump back into it."

Five minutes later, Jenna didn't even realize she was holding her breath until she saw a small blue car tucked in a turnout around the next bend. Her chest deflated and she almost dropped to her knees.

"Do you think that's it? Do you think that's the car?"

"Positive." Cade pulled the key chain from his pocket and aimed the remote at the car. It blinked to life, flashing its lights once and beeping. Cade bounced Gavin a few times and grinned. "Can I say I told you so?"

"You can say whatever you like." She quickened her steps. "Just get me out of here."

Cade popped the trunk of the car and tossed his bag and backpack inside. He swung Gavin from his back. "You did great, kiddo."

Jenna grabbed Gavin's hand and led him to the backseat. "I'll buckle you up. We'll get you a car seat as soon as we can."

Gavin settled in and yanked at the seat belt. "Don't need a car seat."

"Oh, yes, you do. Don't get used to this." She slid into

the passenger seat and snapped on her own seat belt. "Where to?"

"Away."

Cade cranked on the engine and pulled the little car onto the road. "We get as far away from here as we can. Then we'll have some breakfast and regroup."

Jenna looked in the side mirror at the empty road stretching behind them and shook her head. "Unbelievable."

"What? I told you the car would be here."

"Helicopters blowing up, random cars parked in the bushes, a shed full of—" she fluttered hands "—stuff. Is that a typical day in your life?"

He slid a glance her way before studying the road. "No. It happens now and then. We spend a lot of time on intelligence, analyzing data, tracking people through banking, car registration, medical records. Boring stuff."

"That's not working too well for tracking down Zendaris, is it?"

He smacked the steering wheel, his jaw tightening. "He's smart. He has loyal people surrounding him, and when they cease to be loyal…" He fired an imaginary gun with his fingers.

"What else do you know about him besides the fact that he's a vicious killer and has no morals?"

"Not much. He's Greek, comes from a small fishing village on one of the islands. Samos, I think. He left at about age fifteen. Went to Italy. Was involved in some petty crimes there."

"And immediately graduated to arms dealing?"

"He had a few hiccups on the road, but he's one of the biggest arms dealers in the world now. We just can't pin him down."

"But he can find you."

"Guess so."

Jenna slumped in her seat, leaning her head against the window. Would she and Gavin ever be free as long as Zendaris lived? She'd never come close to wishing someone dead, but she wouldn't shed any tears over Zendaris's obituary.

Cade traced a line down the side of her neck, and she closed her eyes, soaking in the small gesture. It ended with his hand on her shoulder.

"I'm going to fix this."

For just a moment, Jenna allowed herself to believe him.

Her gaze flicked to the side mirror. "Do you think they're following us?"

"They'll try, but we got a head start on them, and they're going to have a hard time getting a vehicle onto this road, if they even realize we're on this road."

"So we're safe...for now." She figured she might as well add the words for him.

"We're safe and we're hungry." Cade checked the rearview mirror. "Right, Gavin?"

"Pancakes."

"What happened to eggs?"

"Pancakes," Gavin repeated.

Cade pointed to a gas station out the window. "Looks like we're heading toward civilization. Pancakes can't be far behind."

Another fifty miles down the highway, more gas stations, a few motels and finally a town came into view. And just like Cade had accurately predicted the car waiting for them, he had accurately predicted pancakes in their future.

Maybe he could tell her that she and Gavin would stop running and be right about that, too.

The car careened along the off-ramp past a Native American roadside stand selling blankets and trinkets. "We must be close to Vegas."

"Other side." Cade turned into the small parking lot of a diner. "We went southeast. We're close to the four corners, Colorado to the east of us and New Mexico to the south."

He parked the car and they made for the restaurant. Jenna peered through the glass door at the crowded dining room. "Do you have a plan beyond breakfast?"

"I always have a plan." Cade tapped on the window of the restaurant at a flyer advertising a flea market. "Maybe we can pick up a car seat for Gavin here."

"Maybe I can pick up some clothes." Jenna tugged her jacket around her body. The couple of times she'd packed up and moved, she'd had time to get ready. Her helter-skelter dash from her house in Lovett Peak had been the first time she'd had to put her emergency evacuation plan into action. It had worked pretty well, too, although Zendaris's men may have been able to stop her if it hadn't been for Cade and his muscle...car.

Cade swung open the door, and Jenna nudged Gavin in front of her into the packed restaurant. She scanned the room for suspicious-looking people, although she didn't figure they'd be men in suits and dark glasses. Zendaris hadn't gotten to his position in the world by surrounding himself with stupid people.

But everyone made mistakes.

Cade hung his arm around her shoulders and whispered in her ear. "Relax."

"Table for three?" A waitress gripping a pot of steaming coffee paused by the door, cocking her head at Cade.

"Yes, ma'am."

The woman tilted her chin toward a booth by the window. "You can take that table when the busboy clears it."

Gavin tugged on Jenna's hand and motioned her down to his level. She ducked and touched her nose to his. "What do you need?"

"I need to go potty."

"Right. First things first." She turned to Cade. "I'm going to take Gavin to the restroom."

"I should probably wash my hands, too. Do you want me to take him to the men's room?"

Jenna ignored Gavin's hopeful look. Even at his age, he resented being dragged to the women's restroom all the time. "Uh, he still needs a little help."

"And who's more qualified to help him with guy stuff?" He took Gavin's other hand, gave one tug and Gavin dropped her hand as if a she had a trick buzzer in it.

Gavin galloped beside this stranger he'd met only yesterday, under less-than-ideal circumstances, and Jenna followed them to the restrooms with a lump in her throat.

Bracing her hands on the vanity, she hunched over the sink, taking stock of her reflection. Her hair stuck out at odd angles, and she had a smudge of dirt on one cheek. How long had that been there?

Leave it to a man to miss the important things and dwell on stuff like blowing up helicopters and locating getaway cars.

She cranked on the faucet and scrubbed her hands. Holding her hair back with one hand, she splashed warm water on her face with the other, rubbing at the spot on her cheek.

If she put any makeup on at this point, she'd be sending all the wrong signals to Cade. And what kinds of signals did she want to send him? How long would they be on the run together?

She pawed through her purse and pulled out a tube of lipstick. She swiped the dark pink color across her lips and smacked them twice.

She could handle whatever he threw her way.

Entering the dining room, she spotted Cade and Gavin already sitting at the booth—on the same side of the table.

They had their noses buried in their menus, two dark heads bent side by side.

She slid into the booth across from them. "What looks good?"

Gavin slapped the plastic menu on the table and jabbed his finger at a picture of pancakes with dollops of whipped cream on them in the shape of a happy face. "Pancakes."

"Really?" She wrinkled her nose. "Since when do we eat whipped cream for breakfast?"

Cade raised his menu to cover his face. "Don't look at me. I'm having a breakfast burrito. Your mom knows best, Gavin."

Gavin's lower lip trembled and Jenna felt as if she'd just shot down the Easter bunny. Who was she to nix whipped cream after what she'd just put her son through?

She blew a kiss to Gavin. "Are you getting those with chocolate chips?"

He nodded and bounced in his seat.

Cade peered at her over the top of his menu. "When you go all out, you go all out."

"Hey, if you can't have whipped cream when you're on the…road, when can you have whipped cream?"

The waitress came back and plopped a coloring book and crayons on the table in front of Gavin and took their order.

Jenna wrapped her hands around her coffee cup and inhaled the rich aroma from the steam curling up to her nose. "One sip of this and I might feel halfway human again."

Cade downed his orange juice in a couple of gulps and shoved the small glass to the edge of the table. "You did an amazing job back there in Lovett Peak. I was too late, and you handled yourself well."

"I'm not sure what would've happened if you hadn't come along in that car. They'd put the word out that I had something to do with—" she glanced at Gavin, his tongue lodged in the corner of his mouth as he scribbled red across the page "—Marti. D-do you think I'm wanted or whatever?"

"For questioning, maybe. The police have no evidence."

"She was in my house. I left in a hurry. And they can plant evidence. You should know that."

"I do." He ran his thumb along the ridge of her knuckles. "I'm just sorry you do."

"Don't be sorry. I had to learn fast, and it's kept us alive."

"And happy? What about happiness?"

She jutted out her chin. Did he think she needed him to be happy? That she'd fall apart the minute he left?

"Every time I look at Gavin I'm happy. It's a different sort of life, but it's our life."

"I can see that." He tapped Gavin on the head. "He's a great kid—friendly, happy, fearless."

"Ah, it's that fearless part you like, isn't it? A chip off the old block?"

Cade grinned and scratched the sexy stubble on his chin. "With any luck at all, he'll be an engineer or an accountant. I'd like that, too."

"Maybe he *will* do a one-eighty. People do that, don't they? Choose the opposite path of a parent."

The grin melted from Cade's face, and now his stubble gave him a menacing look. "I guess I didn't. Followed in my old man's footsteps to a T."

Jenna's hand jerked and her coffee sloshed over the rim, splashing her fingers. "What are you talking about? You and your father are complete opposites. You're responsible and honorable. He wasn't."

Cade gazed over her shoulder, his dark eyes clouding over like the sky outside the window. "My father left his family, and so did I."

His words twisted a knife in her gut. Is that what he believed?

Shame washed across her body like a heat wave. Why shouldn't he believe that? She'd been flinging the accusations of abandonment at him ever since she'd jumped in his hot rod.

"It's different." She dragged the tip of her spoon through the coffee puddling in her saucer. "You didn't have a choice. You left for our own safety."

"He didn't have a choice, either." His lips twisted.

"Your father was a criminal, Cade. He left you, your brother and your mother because the Feds were closing in on him."

"Like I said, he didn't have a choice."

The waitress interrupted them with a clatter of plates, and Gavin looked up from his coloring to squeal over the whipped cream face on his chocolate chip pancakes. Jenna might have to pay by enduring hyperactive behavior from him until he crashed, but the look on his wide-eyed face was worth it.

Had to grab pleasure where you could find it.

Gavin poked Cade in the shoulder. "Look, look."

"I see." Cade suspended one long finger above a dollop of cream. "Can I have some?"

Gavin pointed to the smallest dab of whipped cream. "You can have that one."

"Thanks." Cade dipped the tip of his finger into the white puff and sucked it into his mouth. "Yum."

Gavin attacked his stack of pancakes as if he hadn't eaten in days, and Cade sliced into his burrito with equal gusto.

Jenna watched them, her fork suspended over her omelet. Even though he hadn't started life with his father, Gavin shared so many characteristics with Cade—the tilt of his head, the quick smile, the way they both had her wrapped around their fingers.

She sniffed and plunged her fork into her eggs. She'd have to keep her head on straight with these two, but no more blaming Cade for the way fate had played out in their marriage. Their separation had hurt her and she'd wanted to retaliate against Cade, force him to feel her pain. But that wasn't necessary.

He didn't need her to leash him to his pain. He felt it all on his own with no prompting from her. He felt it on a deep, visceral level that she'd never contemplated.

Cade had never wanted to be like his father, and now he felt as if he'd made the same mistakes as the man who had left his family when Cade was just ten years old.

She'd have to do better. They'd all suffered, and somehow they'd find a way out—together.

She did a fair amount of justice to her own breakfast and pushed her plate to the center of the table. "You said you had a plan. Care to share it with me?"

"Sure." Cade picked up a crayon and colored inside the lines of a balloon on the paper. "There's a Prospero outpost in Arizona. It serves to monitor people crossing the U.S.–Mexican border, keeping an eye out for known terrorists."

Jenna cleared her throat. "A-are we going to get some help there?"

"They can help you and Gavin."

Her muscles tensed. "Me and Gavin?"

"They can settle you in a safe location."

Jenna gripped Cade's wrist and leaned in close, gritting her teeth. "No."

Chapter Seven

Jenna's nails dug into his wrist, but Cade didn't flinch. He expected resistance, anger even, from Jenna. But he had to be strong enough to think with his brain, not his heart.

She cupped her hand around her mouth to shield her words from Gavin. "You are *not* dumping us off at some outpost. Even the name is offensive. Outpost. Out of your life. Out of your mind."

He twisted his wrist from her grasp and smothered both of her hands with his. "That's not possible. You and Gavin are on my mind twenty-four seven."

"What are they going to do with us? Stick us in some kind of witness protection program?"

"That's pretty much what you've been in, anyway, Jenna. New town, different identity, Prospero watching over you. Me watching over you. Only this time it will be official and professional and safer than anything you could do on your own."

"It's no way to live, Cade. It's no way for Gavin to live."

The quaver in her voice just about did him in. Squeezing her hands, he said, "It's not going to be forever."

"How close are you to catching Zendaris?"

His eye twitched, and she withdrew her hands from his. "Exactly."

"He's going to find out sooner or later that I don't have those plans and once he does, he'll back off."

"Why would he do that? He's had a vendetta against you for three years. Even if he finds out you don't have the plans, that doesn't wipe out his other grievance. He was after me before you took the plans, and he'll be after me after he finds out you don't have them."

"You missed one." Cade leaned over Gavin's coloring masterpiece and pointed to a flower. When Gavin turned his attention to picking out a crayon for the blank flower, Cade hunched forward, his nose almost touching Jenna's. "Let's just get you safe and settled."

Jenna took a deep breath, held it for a moment and then released it through parted lips. "Okay. We'll go to this outpost. I—I'm not blaming you, Cade. It is what it is."

He managed to prevent his jaw from hitting the table, but he couldn't control his eyebrows, which jumped up to his hairline. Since when was she not blaming him? He'd take it for now.

"Then let's do a little shopping while we're here, at least pick up a few changes of underwear and a couple of shirts. I need to let them know we're on the way, anyway."

"Underwear." Gavin giggled and finished off the flower with an orange flourish.

Cade paid the bill with cash. In fact, he and Jenna had enough cash between them to open their own bank. She'd handled things well on her own, but he didn't want her to be on her own anymore.

They wandered around the town, which happened to be a hub of sorts for tourists heading to Vegas or the Grand Canyon or Utah's National Parks, and picked up some clothes, toiletries and snacks for the drive.

On the road out of town, the flea market loomed ahead of them, a colorful mishmash of goods and humanity. Cade pulled into the dirt parking lot next to the booths. "Do you think we can find a car seat for Gavin here?"

"I think so. Looks like a giant yard sale, and people are always looking to sell baby items."

They mingled with the people shuffling past the stalls and the wares displayed on blankets. The smell of popcorn and cotton candy wafted through the cold air.

Jenna pinched the sleeve of his jacket. "Baby stuff."

They veered toward a vendor with toys arrayed on a table and tiny clothes hanging from a line. Cade fingered a blue one-piece outfit. Had Gavin ever been this small?

"How much for the car seats?" Jenna had ducked between the clothing and nudged one of two car seats with the toe of her boot.

A smile cracked the vendor's weathered face. "For the little boy? Twenty-five for the blue one and forty for the gray one."

"I'll give you thirty for the gray one." Jenna pinched a twenty and a ten in her fingers and held out the money to the old woman.

"Thirty-five."

"You're not supposed to sell used car seats." She thrust the cash at the woman, who snatched it and tucked it into her pocket.

Jenna had become one tough customer. That flighty girl he'd met in Coronado had morphed into a responsible, no-nonsense woman.

Cade hooked the straps of the car seat around his arm and it bumped his leg as they meandered back through the flea market.

The smell of the sugar from the cotton candy must've intoxicated Gavin because he started yanking on Jenna's hand and whining for candy.

"Gavin, you are not getting any candy." She rolled her

eyes at Cade and whispered, "I think he wants cotton candy and that's a double no."

Then he stopped the whining and started skipping and chanting. "Please, Mommy. Please, Mommy. Please, Mommy."

"Would the little one like some homemade cornbread with honey?" A small, gray-haired Native American woman smiled and nodded toward Gavin.

Jenna stopped. "Oh, I suppose so."

Cade chuckled in her ear. "It's better than cotton candy."

"You're the child's mother?"

"Yes." Jenna peered more closely at the old woman's cloudy, unfocused eyes and realized she was blind. "I don't want to trouble you."

"Little ones need something sweet now and then." The old woman turned her head to the side. "Patrick."

A young man stepped from the recesses of the booth, holding a paper plate with a square of cornbread drizzled with honey in the center. "Just one?"

"I think that's enough for us to share. How much?"

Cade stepped forward and took the plate from Patrick. He sawed off a small piece of the cornbread, stabbed it with the plastic fork and fed it to Gavin.

The woman waved her gnarled hands. "Take it, but I'd like to read your cards."

Jenna stumbled back against Cade. "Read my cards?"

The woman slid a stack of cards from the folds of her dress and rapped it against the table. The cards did not come from a regular playing deck. They were composed of some hard substance, and as the woman spread them on the table Jenna saw shapes and figures carved into the cards.

The old woman ran her fingertips along the ridges and grooves of the shapes. She must've had this set of cards created exclusively for her.

"Are those tarot cards?"

She caressed the cards with knotted fingers. "Some call them tarot cards. We call it an oracle deck."

Jenna glanced over her shoulder at Cade and Gavin stuffing cornbread into their mouths, and Cade shrugged.

She slipped into the chair opposite the fortune-teller. "Can you tell my future with that deck?"

"I see—" she drew a hand across her milky eyes "—many things."

Who was she to deny the old woman a chance to practice her art? Jenna folded her hands on the table and took a deep breath. "What do I have to do?"

"Nothing at all." The woman's hushed tones caused the hair on the back of Jenna's neck to quiver.

The woman closed her sightless eyes and fanned the cards in front of her in an array of suns and moons and animals.

Jenna found herself holding her breath as the woman read the cards with her fingertips. She slid them around the table, discarding some and arranging the others in the pattern of a cross.

When she had the oracle cards where she wanted them, she traced the shapes of each one with her fingers. When she finished stroking the final card, she swept them up and stacked them with their discarded mates.

"Well? What did you see?"

The woman's eyes flew open and Jenna flinched at the pale opaque film that seemed to float over both orbs. The seer grabbed Jenna's hand in a clawlike grip.

"You live a life of danger."

Jenna stiffened and she felt Cade move in behind her and slip a hand on her shoulder.

"Someone covets what you have."

Jenna reached out, curling her fingers around Gavin's wrist.

"This person poses the greatest threat to your happiness. Defeat this person, and you shall walk in sunshine."

Jenna's heart hammered in her chest and she hunched forward, staring into the old woman's eyes. "What else? What else did you see?"

"Where is this person? Where can we find him?" Cade's hand tightened on her shoulder.

The young man, Patrick, stepped out from the shadows again and held up his hands. "Reading the oracle deck tires my grandmother. She can't tell you any more."

Despite the chill in the air, a warm flush crept up Jenna's neck. Her voice had risen and she'd been almost nose-to-nose with the woman. She slumped back in her seat as Gavin patted her leg and Cade ran a hand over her hair.

"I'm sorry. I didn't mean to yell at your grandmother."

Patrick collected the cards from the oracle deck and stacked them next to his grandmother's elbow, resting on the table. She appeared to be asleep.

"She doesn't take offense when her readings upset people, but you need to be careful. She picked you out of the crowd."

Squeezing Jenna's shoulder again, Cade asked, "What does that mean?"

The man shrugged. "She felt your aura. She wanted to warn you. She does this to earn a few bucks, but she's never wrong."

With trembling hands, Jenna dug into her bag. "Money. How much do I owe you?"

Patrick waved it off. "She wanted to read the oracle deck for you."

"I insist." Jenna peeled a twenty from her roll of cash. "Is this enough?"

"That's fine, but the highest form of payment for my grandmother is that you heed her words. That's why she singled you out."

Jenna shoved back from the table and the dozing woman. "Believe me, I'm heeding."

Moments later, Jenna tucked Gavin into his new used car seat and slammed the back door.

Cade pinned her to the side of the car, one hand on each shoulder. "That fortune-telling mumbo jumbo is nothing we didn't already know. Don't let it upset you."

"But she could feel the danger coming off me. She couldn't even see me and she felt it."

"Maybe she is for real, but that doesn't change a thing. We know Zendaris is after Gavin. We know you're both in danger."

Cade spoke the truth. What did it matter that some Native American shaman had confirmed what she already knew? Danger swirled around her. Any shaman worth her salt should be able to sense that a mile away.

She blew out a breath and sagged against the car. "You're right. Hearing it spoken aloud like that and by a stranger gave me the heebie-jeebies."

"I get that." Then he leaned in and kissed her on the mouth, short and oh-so-sweet. "We can get to the Prospero outpost by nightfall if we get moving. Lunch on the road."

Cade circled the car to the driver's side, and Jenna had to peel herself from the car door. That man's touch still worked magic. The old woman could just as well have been warning her about Cade. He posed a grave danger and had the ability to take something precious away from her. Her heart.

CADE SLID INTO THE driver's seat wishing he'd kissed her longer and harder. She needed it after that soothsayer had spooked her.

He pulled his phone out of his pocket. "I'm going to go ahead and let the outpost know we're on our way."

"You have the phone number for some outpost in the middle of nowhere?"

He slid the phone open and tapped out a message on the tiny keyboard. "We use a message center. I let them know I'm on my way in, using the outpost's code, and the message gets relayed to the outpost."

"You guys are almost as good James Bond."

He picked up a pen in the console. "But this pen is just a pen."

They'd fallen back into their teasing banter, and she'd taken a break from accusing him of abandonment every ten minutes. Progress. Now how could they get from here to forever after?

Several minutes later his cell phone buzzed and he checked the display. "Confirmation."

"So they know we're on our way and will be rolling out the red carpet?"

"They'll be expecting us, anyway. They know you're with me and maybe can start working on relocating you and Gavin to a safe place."

Jenna sighed and he held his breath, but she didn't respond further. Did she really believe she and Gavin would be safer on their own without Prospero behind them?

Maybe not on their own, but safer with me.

The thought slammed against his brain. He knew he could keep his family safe, and he owed it to them. Jenna may have stopped blaming him for running out on her and Gavin, but he hadn't stopped blaming himself.

Was he putting them in jeopardy again by dumping them off on Prospero? It felt as if he was abdicating his responsibility.

Cade shook his head. Emotion could cloud your judgment. The nameless, faceless techs and analysts with Prospero would be able to make the right decisions based on facts.

Jenna touched his arm. "Are you sure you don't want me to drive?"

Before he could answer, his phone buzzed again. He squinted at the display. "It's Jared."

"Jared Douglas from your team?"

"The one and only." He answered the call because he'd answer any call, any time from J.D., Gage or Deb. "Hey, I heard you were out of the country."

Jared's voice crackled over the line. "I am. I saw your message come through. You're on your way to the Arizona outpost with your family?"

"Yep." Cade punched the button for the speakerphone. Jenna had more at stake than he did and deserved to know everything.

"Give my best to Jenna."

"Do it yourself. You're on speaker."

"Hey, darlin'. Do you still hate me?"

She rolled her eyes at Cade. "Nothing personal, J.D., but you spent more time with my husband than I did after we got married."

He laughed. "Yeah, we had a sweet honeymoon in Afghanistan. But you can have him back."

"Don't provoke her, J.D. She's not the same sweet girl she used to be."

"I could've told you that. The minute I met her, I could tell that little filly was going to take you for a ride."

"Okay, cut the cowboy act, J.D. I know you didn't call just to hear my dulcet tones."

"Just wanted to tell you, I heard from Gage recently. He's following a lead on Zendaris." The line hissed and buzzed as if for emphasis.

Gage Booker had been their other Prospero Three team member, along with the first female agent, Deb Sinclair. The four of them had been responsible for torpedoing Zendaris's first big arms deal.

"How close is he, J.D.?" Cade reached over and squeezed Jenna's fingers. "We need to bring him down now more than ever."

Jared's voice faded in and out. "Did you hear me? Gage is working on an informant, someone who worked for Zendaris in South America."

"Does he have the informant in hand?"

Dead air met his question.

"J.D.? Does Gage have the informant?"

"Not yet."

"He'd better get on it. We all know how quickly Zendaris's former employees disappear."

"Don't I know it. Gage knows it, too. He's treating this one with kid gloves."

"The sooner we nail that SOB, the better for everyone."

"Especially if those plans for the anti-drone fall into his hands again." Jared coughed, or was it the phone again? "No word on the plans yet, huh?"

"Disappeared like one of Zendaris's former employees."

"I wonder why they haven't…"

J.D.'s last words were garbled, but Cade filled in the blanks and his muscles tensed. "Are you accusing me of something, bro?"

Even through the static, Jared's voice took on an edge. "You know me better than that. I'm just sayin'…"

"What? What are you saying?" His grip had tightened on Jenna's fingers, and she squirmed out of his hold. "What are you trying to tell me, J.D.?"

"Watch…back. Zendaris…not…only one after…"

Chapter Eight

Jenna couldn't breathe. J.D.'s words had left them hanging. The line had gone completely dead.

"What did he mean? What was he trying to say? Zendaris is not the only one after the plans or not the only one after you?"

"You heard as much as I did." Cade wiped his brow and turned down the heater in the car.

"Does he believe other arms dealers might be after you?"

Cade gulped some water from the bottle in the cup holder. "It's like your fortune-teller, Jenna. J.D. didn't tell us anything we didn't already know. People are after me. People are after you and Gavin. We need to watch our backs. That's why we're going to settle you in a safe location."

"Maybe Gage Booker will get lucky with this informant."

"Gage was born lucky. If anyone can get a line on Zendaris, it's Gage." He touched her smooth cheek. "Then this relocation can come to an end, and we can start our life together."

She pursed her lips and turned up the radio. They'd have to discuss that further—and riding in a car on the way to some Prospero stronghold was not the time or the place.

The dry landscape unfolded before them as they rolled

down the highway. They'd stopped for a lunch of fast food, which Gavin had devoured as if he hadn't eaten in days.

When Cade turned off the highway, Jenna sat up and peered into the darkness that had fallen over the desert like a curtain at the end of a play. "Are we here?"

"Almost."

"Then what?"

"We can get some rest, and then Prospero will start working on new identities for you and Gavin. They may have already started. Beth Warren is one of the best researchers in this area. She'll find a place where you two can blend in and stay safe."

"That's if I agree to go." She clenched her teeth and hardened her jaw. "I'm not under arrest or anything. I can do what I want."

He drummed his thumbs against the steering wheel. "Of course you can, but you'll do what's best for Gavin."

"And that is?"

"Taking him to a secure location."

"Where would that be?" She glanced over her shoulder at her sleeping son. "I've been looking for that place for three years."

"That's what we're going to figure out. Let's leave it to the professionals."

Cade drove in silence for several more minutes and made another turn. The headlights of the car picked out a squat building that could blend in with the golds and russets of the landscape during the daytime. The building seemed to rise from the sand. Low lights illuminated the narrow windows, which glinted in the oncoming lights.

Jenna tapped the window. "That's the outpost?"

"It is. You'd be amazed at what goes on in there."

"They still can't locate Zendaris."

"We can leave that to Gage." Cade aimed the car down a

long dirt drive toward the building, and the tires crunched and crackled. "They have a different mission here. They're not after Zendaris. He's out of their scope."

"Apparently he's out of everyone's scope."

"Not for long. We'll get him. He wants those plans back in the worst way, and he's going to make a mistake trying to get them. When he makes that mistake, Prospero will be there, and if Gage gets an informant, we'll be there even sooner."

He pulled around the back of the building where a few other cars were parked and stopped next to a Jeep.

"Are you sure they know we're coming?" Jenna studied the back of the building, unlit and unwelcoming.

"I got the confirmation that they received my message."

As Cade got out of the car, Jenna turned in her seat and grabbed the toe of Gavin's boot. She jiggled his foot up and down. "Hey, sleepyhead. We're here. Wake up."

Gavin mumbled and rubbed his eyes. "Are we eating?"

"Again? You're an eating machine."

Cade swung open the back door. "Are you ready to come out of there?"

Gavin nodded and Cade released the buckle, peeling the straps from Gavin's shoulders. Cade scooped him out of the car seat.

And hitched him up on one hip…like a natural.

Jenna ground her teeth together. She had to stop thinking like that. Tomorrow morning, he'd be sending her and Gavin packing. For their own good, of course.

Cade stepped away from the door and tilted his head back, waving at the eaves. He winked at Jenna. "Camera."

The heavy door clicked and a piece of the door slid up, revealing a compartment. Cade rubbed the palm of his right hand against his jeans and placed it inside the cavity. A row of lights blinked red and then turned green.

The door clicked again, and Cade produced a card from his pocket and slid it into a slot next to the compartment. One more click and Cade pushed open the door.

"High tech." Jenna raised her brows as she brushed past him into the building.

The heavy door slammed behind them, leaving them in a short, dark hallway lined with closed doors.

Cade drew his brows over his nose. "Where is everyone?"

Jenna shuffled closer to Cade and curled her hand around Gavin's leg dangling against Cade's thigh. "Is there usually a welcoming committee?"

"I've been here only once before, but typically the agents working at these outposts pop their heads out because they don't get many visitors."

As if on cue, one of the doors swung open and a young man wearing wire-rimmed glasses peered around its edge. "Agent Stark?"

Cade crossed his arms. "Is that protocol around here? Shouldn't you make me identify myself?"

The man's face reddened and he blinked. "Yeah, sorry. We don't get a lot of agents out this way. I've seen your picture before, and I did notice your palm print verified."

"Were you watching me on camera to make sure it wasn't someone else placing my dead hand on the reader?"

Jenna sucked in a breath. She hadn't thought of that, but apparently the bespectacled man had.

"Yes, I was watching you on camera from the minute the car pulled into the back lot." He stuck out his hand. "Horace Jimerson. Everyone calls me *Jim*."

"Cade Stark, and this is my wife, Jenna, and my son, Gavin."

The men shook hands, and then Jim offered his hand to Jenna. He squeezed her fingers in a bony grip and she hoped he didn't plan to apply the same pressure to Gavin's little hand.

But he patted Gavin on top of the head instead. "If you're hungry, we have a communal kitchen in the back."

"Is Greg Miyata still stationed here?"

"Miyata? Yeah, he's still here."

"Good. I was hoping he could help with the resettlement of my wife and son until this thing gets sorted out. Is Beth Warren on the job yet?"

Jim slipped off his glasses and wiped the lenses on his wrinkled shirt. "I'm afraid I don't know much about the specific plans. Zendaris, right?"

"Uh-huh."

"That means I really don't have any of the details, Agent Stark. You field ops are hush-hush about that guy."

"Call me Cade." He took a turn around the hallway, his gaze skimming past all the closed doors. "So where's Miyata and the other techs?"

"Miyata's out right now—overnight assignment at the border, and Sonia Pacheco, the only other tech here, is sleeping. She had the early morning shift." Jim glanced over his shoulder into the room behind him. "I need to get back to something. The kitchen's at the end of the hall. Help yourself. You and your family can have the sleeping quarters in the last room on the right. Miyata will have more information when he returns."

Cade hoisted a groggy Gavin in his arms. "Get back to work. We'll figure it out. Will Miyata be back tomorrow?"

"Should be. I'll join you in about an hour." Jim almost jumped at a beep from one of the computers behind him.

Cade trudged down the sterile hallway with Jenna close on his heels.

"This is a strange place." She sidled closer to him, which he didn't mind in the least. "Do the techs live here?"

"Yeah, they live here, but they're not chained to their desks. They're close enough to the border that they probably make runs there for assignments." He pulled open the door at the end of the hallway and a strong smell of antiseptic cleaner made his eyes water.

Jenna wrinkled her nose. "At least they keep it clean."

Cade settled Gavin in a chair at a small table in the middle of the white-on-white room, and he immediately sank his head into his folded arms.

Jenna crouched beside him, running her hand over his close-cropped hair. "Do you want a snack before bedtime?"

Gavin answered by burrowing his head farther into the crook of his arm.

Pausing with his hand on the refrigerator, Cade said, "Should we try to entice him with some food or put him to bed right now?"

"I think he's okay where he is." She joined him at the open fridge. "I can use one of those diet sodas."

"I can use one of those beers." He wrapped his hand around a frosty bottle and twisted off the lid.

"It's kind of creepy here, isn't it?" Jenna snapped the tab of the can and slurped at the foam that bubbled to the rim.

Cade dragged his gaze away from her puckered lips. "It's isolated, but we passed a town on the way in and Phoenix isn't far."

"Maybe Gavin and I should hide in plain sight."

"What does that mean?"

She pulled out a chair next to Gavin and dropped into it. "I always stuck to smaller towns, but maybe blending into a big city would work better."

"I don't know." He leaned a shoulder against the fridge. "I think your instincts were right. Strangers stand out more in small towns. In a big city, anyone could move in and out of the neighborhood and you wouldn't be able to keep track. Beth will have it figured out."

Scooting her chair back, she rested her head against Gavin's, light against dark. "I'm tired of thinking about stuff like that."

He shrugged off the refrigerator and squatted between his wife and son, wrapping an arm around each of them. "I know. This is going to end soon. I can feel it. And then…"

She turned and pinned him with her blue gaze. "And then what?"

He fell forward on his knees and cupped her face in his hands. "And then we'll be together, like we were always meant to be."

He kissed her mouth harder than he'd intended, but she didn't back away. When had Jenna ever backed away from anything?

She returned his kiss with a fire that he'd felt only in his dreams. Sliding from her chair, she perched half on its edge, half on his knee. Her unexpected weight toppled him backward and he sprawled on the linoleum floor with his wife on top of him.

They both laughed, and Jenna's smile brightened his whole world. Right in that instant, he knew he'd move mountains to be with her again—move mountains and relentlessly pursue an arms dealer to the ends of the earth.

The door to the kitchen swung open and Jim cleared his throat. "Sorry."

Jenna rolled from Cade's body, leaving a burning ache in his belly. "Don't mind us. We're just testing out the cleanliness of the place."

Jim narrowed his eyes behind his glasses. The guy had a buttoned-down personality that suited his environment. No wonder Prospero had placed him out here.

Cade hopped to his feet. "She's just kidding."

"Yeah, yeah. We have to live here, so we try to keep it clean. Did you find anything to eat?"

"We ate on the road." Cade chugged down some more beer. "But this sure hits the spot."

"That's Miyata's. I don't drink here on the job."

Cade shrugged. "Like you said, you have to live here."

"Are you sure you're not hungry?" Jim tugged open the refrigerator and pulled out a bowl of what looked like pasta. "We have some leftovers. Sonia's a pretty good cook."

"Sure, you let the little lady do the cooking." Jenna winked at Cade.

This joke went straight over Jim's head, too. "Sonia likes to cook, but Miyata and I have our specialties, too. Sonia is our language specialist. She's fluent in Spanish, but she knows Arabic, French and Italian, too. She does more than cooking."

"That was a joke, Jim."

"Can't be too careful with all the sexual harassment and discrimination lawsuits flying around."

"I'm sure you're a model of decorum out here." Jenna had a smirk in her voice that she kept off her face, but Cade could recognize because she'd aimed it at him enough times.

Jim popped the lid on the plastic bowl of leftover pasta. "It'll take two minutes in the microwave."

Cade held up his hands. Jimbo was relentless. "That's okay. We're good."

"Your son? He probably won't like the pasta, but we have a couple of frozen pizzas."

Jenna balanced her chin on Gavin's shoulder and kissed his cheek. "He's sleeping."

"Sleeping quarters outside to the left, Jim?" Cade leaned forward and scooped Gavin from the chair. Gavin nestled his head in the hollow between Cade's neck and shoulder, and Cade felt as if he could hold his son like this all night.

Zendaris had a lot to answer for.

"To the left." Jim scurried forward and pushed open the kitchen door.

Jenna followed Cade out of the kitchen and opened the door Jim indicated.

Two made-up beds were positioned on either side of the room. Unless Jenna insisted on sleeping in Gavin's bed, it looked as if Cade was going to spend the night in the same bed with his wife for the first time in three years. The floor of the cabin didn't count.

Cade tucked Gavin into the bed away from the door and placed his little boots on the floor at the foot of the bed. "Probably should've brushed his teeth first."

Jenna tugged the covers more securely around Gavin's shoulders. "It happens sometimes. I think our circumstances warrant a disruption in his schedule."

Cade dimmed the lights, propped open the door and then kicked down the stopper on the kitchen door. He and Jenna joined Jim, sitting at the table, the uneaten bowl of pasta in front of him.

Guess Sonia wasn't such a great cook, after all.

Cade sat in the chair across from Jim and stretched his legs in front of him. "Do you have any news?"

"Not about Zendaris." Jim pinched the bridge of his nose. "We do have a pile of Korans picked up along the border, but ICE hasn't brought anyone in who can claim ownership."

"You said Miyata's at the border? Is that what he's looking at?"

"Yes. He's inspecting some items the Border Patrol agents confiscated. He does that a lot."

"We need a place to stay for the night, anyway." Cade

folded his hands behind his head. "Maybe Sonia can help us, too. She's an analyst like Miyata, right? I'm figuring you for the computer geek."

Jim straightened his glasses. "I am the computer *tech*. I think you should wait for Miyata's return, though. You know him from before and he can work with Beth Warren."

"Can you call him on your secure cell?"

"We don't get any reception out here. It's not only the location but the thick walls of the compound."

"So Miyata doesn't know we're here?"

"No. Sonia and I were the only ones here when we got the message of your arrival. I didn't even attempt to contact Miyata. Despite what you experienced when you walked into the hallway, we try to follow protocol out here. We have to. The other side is always watching, always ready."

Cade scraped the label from his beer bottle. "Have you heard anything about the missing plans? Any chatter?"

"We figured you still had them." Jim's eyes, magnified by his thick lenses, blinked.

Jenna gasped, echoing Cade's own sentiments precisely.

"Really?" Cade had to catch the bottle before it toppled to the table. "Who's *we*? Who believes that?"

Jim's gaze darted back and forth between him and Jenna, a dangerous glitter in her eyes. *Good to know she still believed in him.*

Jim licked his lips before he spoke. "A lot of people. Some are saying you still have the plans and are trying to throw Zendaris off."

"If I had the plans—" Cade planted his clammy palms on the table in front of him "—I would've turned them over to the government by now. Why would I hold on to them?"

"Why does Zendaris think you're holding on to them? Let's face it, once the U.S. government has those plans, Zendaris's cause is lost. He's not going to get them back from the government. So he must believe you have them and intend to keep or sell them."

Cade's hands curled into fists. "It's one thing for Zendaris to think I have other intentions for those plans, but why would anyone in Prospero think I do?"

"I'm just the messenger." Jim held up his soft, uncalloused hands.

Cade growled his response. "The next time you hear that garbage, set 'em straight."

"How *did* you lose those plans?"

Jenna slapped the table. "He didn't *lose* them. Someone *stole* them."

Jenna's defense of him acted like a cool salve to his thumping, hot anger. His wife really did have his back.

"How did it happen?" Jim shrugged apologetically as Cade shifted forward in his seat. "We don't hear much out in the boonies."

"I lifted the plans, which were on a flash drive, from Zendaris's courier in an alley in Zurich. I brought the drive back to my hotel, plugged it into my laptop—my secure government laptop—and two hours later, they had disappeared from that same laptop."

Jenna's jaw dropped, and Jim's eyes got even bigger behind his glasses.

Jenna recovered first. "I didn't realize you'd had them for only two hours."

"It was probably less than two hours if you want to know the truth."

"Who knew you were going to lift those plans?" Jim hunched forward as if conducting his own interrogation.

"When I intercepted the courier, I think he recognized me. Maybe Zendaris had alerted him to all of us—those of us on Prospero Team Three. Anyway, I left him in the alley."

"Dead?"

"No. I had what I wanted."

Jim snapped his fingers. "If you didn't kill the courier, maybe he's the one who hacked into your laptop."

"Two hours later? I don't think so. I said I didn't leave him for dead." Cade raised one brow. "That doesn't mean all his parts and faculties were in working order."

Jenna crossed her arms and hunched her shoulders, digging her fingertips into her upper arms.

Cade bit the inside of his cheek. He didn't like exposing Jenna to the seamier side of his job, but then she'd lived that seamier side every day since she'd been on the run.

"Then who knew you had the plans? You can understand why people might not believe you—not that I don't." Jim shoved back from the table and stretched. "You two can bunk in the room with your son. I'm going to get back to work."

He left the door ajar and his sneakers squished down the hallway.

Cade blew out a breath. "Wow, I didn't realize I was under suspicion."

"That's Jim's take on it." Jenna waved her hands in an airy gesture. "Do you really think Prospero would be allowing you to roam around the country a free agent if they really suspected you of having that flash drive?"

"Some people within Prospero must have their suspicions."

Jenna prowled around behind his chair and dug her fingers into his shoulders. "Not the important people. If Jack Coburn suspected you, he'd be interrogating you right now."

Closing his eyes, Cade rolled back his head, giving in to the pressure of Jenna's fingers now squeezing the tension from the back of his neck. "Jack even knows about my father, and he still trusts me with intelligence."

Jenna's thumbs stalled at the base of his skull before she burrowed beneath his hair. "Your father has nothing to do with drugs or weapons."

"But he's a crook."

"And you're not."

"Do you think that's what the rest are saying about me? Like father, like son? Gage's father was practically military royalty. J.D.'s dad a salt-of-the-earth rancher and Deb's dad, well, she didn't know her father. They all probably think Jack was a fool to overlook my past."

The slap on the side of his head brought tears to his eyes, and he ducked out of Jenna's reach. "Hey!"

She leaned to the side, meeting his eyes. "There's more where that came from if you don't stop talking nonsense."

"You spoiled the massage." He rubbed his knuckles across his scalp.

"We can continue later." She swept the bowl of pasta from the counter and stuck it in the sink. "What time do you think Miyata will be back tomorrow?"

"I have no idea. We might have to work with Sonia. I'm sure she can help us out."

Jenna plucked the lid from the bowl and turned on the faucet. "You're sure you don't want some of this food?"

"No, thanks. I have a suspicion it's bad since Jim was trying so hard to pawn it off on us."

She aimed the faucet into the bowl. "I'll get rid of it because it's been sitting out for a while."

Cade pushed out of the chair and stretched. Then he tossed his empty beer bottle into the recycling bin. "Gee, do you think a recycling truck comes all the way out here?"

"Can't Prospero command anything?" She brushed past him and pushed open the door.

Cade flicked off the kitchen lights and followed her back to the room where Gavin was sleeping. One room, two beds. Would Jenna crowd into Gavin's bed? Or would she take a chance with him?

She stood in the center of the small space, knotting her hands in front of her.

Cade pointed to a door off the room. "That's a bathroom. No shower, but we can at least brush our teeth and wash some travel grit from our bodies. You first."

"Thanks. I guess we have to take what we can get. Can't expect a Prospero outpost in the middle of nowhere to have the same standards as a luxury hotel. Not that I wouldn't take a luxury hotel right now—manicure, facial, Jacuzzi."

Jenna's nervous babble meant her thoughts were running along the same lines as his—sleeping arrangements. He'd just have to settle it when he finished washing up.

He shoved open the bathroom door and gestured inside. "Luxury awaits you—Prospero style."

Jenna hunched over the sink, staring at her reflection. She could share a bed with Cade. They'd been married almost four years. Perfectly natural.

She snorted. There was nothing natural about their marriage. But the sex? As natural as breathing.

Or it used to be.

What did she know now? Had he been as celibate as she during their three-year hiatus? Had he stayed true to their marriage vows across the distance of space and time?

Leaning over the sink, she splashed water on her face. She wanted him again, but this sterile building in the middle of the desert in the middle of the night in the middle of a grand escape was not the time or place.

If not now, when? When would they be together again?

She grabbed the white towel from the ring and buried her face in its freshly laundered scent. Then she balanced her wet toothbrush on the edge of the sink.

She squared her shoulders and swept back into the bedroom. She gulped when she saw Cade already stretched out on the other bed, his boots kicked off, his hands behind his head.

He opened one eye. "I'm tempted to fall asleep right here without brushing my teeth. Would I go down in your estimation if I did? I mean, any further?"

"I wouldn't blame you. We've been on a nonstop roller coaster."

He yawned and shook his head. "Now I'm awake and there's no way I can go to sleep without brushing my teeth."

He rolled from the bed and padded to the bathroom on bare feet. "Be right back."

Jenna eyed the large indentation in the mattress. He hadn't suggested she crawl in with Gavin.

She perched on the edge of the bed and bounced a few times. She swung her legs on top and punched a pillow against the headboard. Sitting up against it, she clasped her hands between her knees—and waited.

Cade crept from the bathroom so silently she didn't notice him until he was crouched beside Gavin's bed. "Does he always sleep this soundly?"

"He's probably exhausted. He usually wakes up a few times during the night."

"We'll have to be quiet, then." Cade shrugged out of his flannel shirt and peeled the T-shirt from his body.

Jenna's heart skipped a couple of beats. Did he have to do that? She drew her knees up to her chest, wrapping her arms around her legs.

Cade hung his clothes over the back of the only chair in the room, and Jenna licked her dry lips. *Make up your mind, already.*

He strolled to the bed and tested the mattress with his hand. "Okay if I join you? We *are* still married."

Jenna released a measured breath through her nose. "Sure. Of course."

Flicking back the covers, Cade slid into the bed next to her. The heat from his skin warmed her body, even though he hadn't made a move to touch her.

She stretched out her legs and rolled to her side—facing away from him. Two seconds later, his hand curled around her waist. He nuzzled the back of her neck and breathed into her ear. "God, I missed you."

She stilled, her breath shallow, tears stinging her eyes. "I missed you, too, Cade, but..."

"Shh." He flattened his hand against her belly. "I don't expect everything to be the way it was."

He tugged her back against his chest, careful not to line up the rest of their bodies. Then he kissed the edge of her ear. "Go to sleep."

Jenna believed that to be an impossible task, but she must've drifted off because she woke with a start, her heart pounding. She shifted onto her back, feeling Cade's solid form next to her.

"Mommy!"

Gavin's whisper brushed across her face and she reached out, her hands groping for his little body in the dark. "What's wrong?"

His lips touched her ear. "There's a lady sleeping. She looks funny."

Her eyes adjusted to the gloom and zeroed in on Gavin leaning over the side of the bed, his face a white circle in the darkness. "Where's the lady?"

His arm shot out behind him. "Out there."

Jenna glanced over her shoulder at Cade, his chest rising and falling with each slow, measured breath. "Why are you wandering around?"

"I was looking for you." He covered his mouth over a giggle bubbling to his lips. "Didn't see you."

"Did you wake up the lady?" Great, she had her son in a top secret facility and he was creeping around startling analysts.

He hunched his shoulders. "She looked funny."

Jenna patted the bed, and Gavin hopped up next to her. "A lot of people look funny when they're sleeping. Why were you bothering her?"

"Looking for you."

"Well, you found me." She wrapped her arms around him. "I was right here all along. You didn't wake her, did you?"

"No. She was bleeding."

Jenna caught her breath. "Bleeding?"

Gavin tapped his mouth. "Right here."

Was Gavin making this up? She slid a glance at Cade and then sat up, scooting toward the edge of the bed. "Can you show me?"

Gavin grabbed her hand and tugged her toward the door. On silent, bare feet, they tiptoed into the hallway. One door on the corridor stood ajar. Gavin must've left it open.

Jenna crept toward the open door as goose bumps raced across her flesh. She poked her head into the room, laid out exactly like the one she'd just left. One bed stood empty. The other held a sleeping form.

"It's someone sleeping, Gavin."

"Uh-huh. With blood."

In the darkness, Jenna's gaze picked out the shape of the person in the bed. One arm dangled to the floor. Could she really be injured?

With Gavin clinging to her side, Jenna shuffled toward the bed. She crouched to peer into the woman's face.

Nausea clawed through Jenna's gut and beads of sweat broke out on her forehead.

The woman's mouth hung open in a silent scream, blood and foam speckling the sheets.

Jenna's mouth yawned open to deliver her own scream, but she never got the chance. A large hand shoved the scream back down her throat.

Chapter Nine

Jenna dug her fingernails into the arm that had her in a vise from behind.

"Jenna, it's me." Cade's harsh whisper weakened her knees. He slipped his hand from her mouth. "Keep quiet."

Turning into his chest, she said, "I think she's dead."

"She *is* dead. Poisoned."

"How do you know that?"

"The smell. I can smell it on her."

"Why? What happened? We need to warn Jim."

Cade gripped her shoulders, his long fingers pinching her. "We're not going near Jim."

She widened her eyes and pulled Gavin against her legs. "What are you saying, Cade?"

"It's Jim. The pasta."

Pressing her fist against her lips, she shook her head. "No, no."

"Listen to me." He cupped her face in his hands. "We're getting out of here. Quietly. God knows where Miyata is."

He hoisted Gavin into his arms and put a finger to his lips. "We're sneaking out of here, Gavin."

The three of them slipped out of Sonia's room and back into their own. Amid heavy breathing, they stuffed their feet into their boots, grabbed the few bags they had and hunched into their jackets.

Cade pushed open the door and looked both ways, as his weapon dangled at his side. He motioned for Jenna to follow him.

Hugging Gavin tightly to her body, she followed Cade into the hallway. He jerked his thumb toward the back of the building, where they'd entered hours ago expecting a safe refuge.

Did that even exist?

Cade pulled Jenna next to him while looking over his shoulder. When he rounded the corner, he stopped, a curse on his lips.

Jim stood in front of the door, holding a gun at an odd angle in front of him. "I guess you forgot about the cameras all over this place. I told you I always watched the cameras."

Cade raised his own weapon and had the satisfaction of watching Jim's face blanch. "I didn't forget. Just hoped you wouldn't be keeping watch."

"No chance of that. Your kid's too valuable for inattention."

Jenna hissed beside him, and Cade nudged her. "You're working for the other side now?"

"I have no love for the other side." Jim's lips hardened to a straight line.

"Just a love of money?"

"It's a matter of being appreciated. Zendaris pays well."

Cade shifted his stance, coiling his muscles. "But there's always a price. Do you think someone like Zendaris is going to let you live when he finds out you had my son and wife and let them slip through your fingers?"

Jim licked his lips. "Not going to happen. He'll pay well when I deliver your son to him."

"I told you, Jimbo, I don't have the plans."

Jim laughed, an odd, hiccupping sound. "I don't believe that story. Nobody believes it."

"You do know what those plans are for, don't you?" Cade took another step closer while trying to block Jenna and Gavin from Jim's line of fire.

"They're for a weapon that will neutralize our drones. Prospero doesn't deign to tell me anything, but Zendaris does."

"Those drones are among our best weapons against terrorism." Cade had to take a deep breath. He couldn't let his rage affect his concentration. "That doesn't bother you?"

"We'll develop other weapons, better weapons."

"And you'll have your money." Cade had already released the safety on his gun, and his finger caressed the trigger. "You killed Sonia. What did you do with Miyata?"

"He really is at the border, but he had no idea you were coming. I didn't tell him. He was here when the message came through, but I let him go on his assignment without telling him." Jim's gun wavered. "Now send your kid over here and I'll let your wife go."

Cade laughed. "Why didn't you try anything before now, Jimbo? You poisoned Sonia and tried to do the same with us. You figured you couldn't take out Sonia any other way, is that it? You're waiting for someone, aren't you? You told them we're here."

Jenna sucked in a quick breath beside him.

"The poison wouldn't have killed you, just incapacitated you."

"That's what I'm saying. You need me incapacitated before you can try anything. Well, guess what?" He clutched his weapon with both hands and pointed it Jim's head. "I'm not incapacitated."

"I'll shoot you, Stark, and your wife and your kid." He drew a cross with his weapon. "I'll just start shooting and I won't care who I hit."

As Jim's gun tracked to the left, Cade squeezed off a

shot and backed Jenna and Gavin against the wall. The blast echoed and a second shot followed it.

But Jim had already dropped to his knees and his bullet hit the plaster of the wall.

Cade gave Jenna a shove. "Get back around the corner."

Blood soaked Jim's shoulder as he tried to gain control of the weapon in his hand, but his hand wouldn't cooperate.

Cade ran at him in a crouched position and then kicked the gun from his unsteady hand. He then landed his boot in the center of Jim's chest, sending him plummeting backward.

Cade scooped up Jim's hot gun from the floor and held his own to Jim's head. He grabbed the collar of Jim's shirt and dragged him into the corner of the hallway.

"Cade! Are you all right?"

"It's okay, Jenna. We're getting out of here." He shot Jim again in the kneecap, and the other man wailed.

"What are you doing?" Jim covered his head with his arms. "I demand to be arrested. I demand to be turned over to the CIA."

Cade peeled his lips back from his teeth in a snarl. The man's cowardice made him almost as sick as his treachery. "I want to make sure you can't let your buddies into the compound when they get here. There's too much valuable intelligence, even though I wouldn't mind letting Zendaris's men get a crack at you once they figure out you let my family slip through your hands."

"Wh-who said Zendaris's men are on their way?" Jim gasped and clutched his leg.

"We didn't fall for the poisoned pasta you used on Sonia, but that didn't concern you because you had a backup. You don't have the stomach or the skill to take out a Prospero agent."

Jim's face reddened, almost matching the blood soaking

his pant leg. "You're not fooling anyone, Stark. You compromised your family's safety for glory by stealing those plans from Zendaris, whether you still have them or not."

"You compromised your country's safety for money. What does that make you?"

"You don't have to prove yourself to this man." Jenna tugged on his arm. "If Zendaris's men are on their way, we need to get out of here."

Cade ran the back of his hand across his sweat-soaked brow, and then he pushed to his feet. He hustled Jenna and Gavin toward the door and turned for one last look at Jim. "I'm sending Prospero out here and a warning to Miyata. If you're lucky, they'll arrive before Zendaris's thugs."

Cade exited the compound after Jenna and made sure the door was closed and sealed. They bundled Gavin into his car seat and Cade sped away from the Prospero outpost, his weapon in his lap.

He fumbled for his phone and punched in the warning message for a compromised compound with an enemy on the way. Then he used a text message to tell the Prospero message center that Jimbo was a traitor, Sonia dead and Miyata in danger if he returned to the outpost.

He waited for the response, hands clutching the steering wheel. When his phone buzzed, he lunged for it and read the message. The single word, *confirmed,* as cold and clinical as it was, made his breathing come easier and the rate of his heart slow down.

Cade drove several miles before either of them said a word to each other. Jenna had been turned in her seat, soothing Gavin, and Cade had been busy looking in all directions for suspicious vehicles. He almost welcomed the opportunity to meet Zendaris's men head-on. It wouldn't stop Zendaris, but he'd have to send fresh meat.

"Jim must've been a traitor all along." Jenna settled back

in her seat and hugged herself around the middle. "When you let him know we were coming in, he saw his opportunity and grabbed it."

"Unfortunately, it's not a rare occurrence. We have moles. They have moles."

"But to murder his coworkers like that—because Zendaris's thugs would've killed Miyata when he returned." She hunched forward, touching her forehead to her knees.

Cade ran a hand along her back. "He didn't consider Miyata and Sonia his coworkers. They represent the enemy."

"Do you think Jim was an ideological traitor or did he do it for money?"

"Does it matter?"

"I guess not." She turned in her seat again and pulled a blanket over Gavin, who was already nodding off. "Where to now?"

"We're heading to Albuquerque. It's a big enough city."

"Is it safe there?"

"What do I know?" He smacked the steering wheel with both hands. "I thought a Prospero outpost would be safe."

She flicked his ear. "Don't start that. Of course you figured a Prospero outpost would be safe."

"Ow." He rubbed his ear. "How's Gavin?"

She twisted in her seat and patted their son. "He's falling asleep."

"I mean, how did he handle all the commotion back there?"

"The gunshots scared him. He covered his ears, but everything happened so fast I don't think he realized what was going on."

"He's our hero. If he hadn't seen Sonia and told you about her, we'd still be sleeping in our beds—sitting ducks for Zendaris's men."

She walked her fingertips along his thigh. "You're our

hero, Cade. You've gotten us out of every jam since we started this journey."

"Now you have two guys looking out for you." He jerked his thumb at the backseat. "You don't have to do this alone anymore, Jenna."

"You're going to have to get rid of Zendaris to remove the threat completely, aren't you? It's not just the plans he wants. He wants revenge against you."

"True, but finding out I don't have the plans will slow him down. His first order of business is getting those back and putting them up for bid on the world market."

"He'd sell them to anyone, wouldn't he?"

"Yep."

"Even the U.S.?"

"We don't operate that way."

She blew out a breath. "Who developed the plans in the first place and who says he doesn't have a million copies of them?"

"The engineer who developed the prototype of the anti-drone now works for us."

Her nails dug into the denim of his jeans. "How did that happen?"

"Let's just say we persuaded him to work for the good guys."

"Persuaded?" She slid a glance his way. "Did we persuade him the same way Zendaris is trying to persuade you to give back the plans?"

"That's not my area."

Jenna shook her head. "When did it become okay to use people's families in matters of war?"

He pressed one finger to her lips. "We don't know if that's how it went down. Maybe we just offered him a better life here. He's now working with us on ways to neutralize the anti-drone in case someone does develop it."

"How did Zendaris get his hands on this man's work?"

"The guy developed it for Zendaris."

"Voluntarily?"

"You're like a dog with a bone."

"I just want to gauge our chances against this guy."

He brought her hand to his lips and kissed the ends of her fingers. "And I just want to get you and Gavin out of his way and off his radar. We have a few hours until we hit Albuquerque. Try to sleep like your son back there."

Jenna yawned. "I can do that. Where are we going once we get there?"

"How about a hotel like normal people?"

She closed her eyes and slouched sideways. "Normal? What's that?"

Once they got through this, Cade intended on giving her normal for the rest of her life...if that's what she wanted.

JENNA TURNED HER HEAD from side to side, rubbing her neck. She pressed her nose against the car window and drank in the sight of city streets. Even slightly deserted city streets beat the unrelenting emptiness of the desert.

"We made it to Albuquerque." She poked her head in the backseat to peer at a sleeping Gavin. "Did he wake up at all?"

"No. I think I would've had to wake you up if he had."

She straightened in her seat and stretched her arms over her head, placing her hands flat against the top of the car. "He's getting used to you."

"I think so, too. When are we going to tell him about me?"

His question knocked the wind out of her. "I—I don't know."

"I think the sooner the better. He's three. He seems to

have accepted a lot in his short life. What's one more surprise? And I hope it's a good one."

"You're right. At three, he's not going to experience much angst over a father popping up out of nowhere."

Cade rolled his eyes. "That's one way of putting it. Has he asked about me much?"

"Here and there."

"And your answer?"

Cade seemed to be holding his breath, and she didn't blame him after the reception she'd given him. "I said you were busy with work."

His chest heaved. "That's not too bad. Now I'm not busy with work. You never showed him any pictures of me?"

"I have, but for obvious reasons I didn't prominently display them anywhere we lived. Why do you doubt that I did?"

"He didn't recognize me when I came on the scene."

"He's three, Cade. I wouldn't expect him to recognize you from those pictures."

He wheeled the car around the next corner and pulled into the parking lot of a big hotel. "We're here, Mrs. Cramer."

"I can be Mrs. Cramer."

"Good because I have ID and credit cards as Robert Cramer. I think we can hang out here for a few days—sleep in real beds, eat real food."

"Buy real clothes." Between two fingers, she pinched the fabric of the cheap jeans she'd bought at the flea market.

"Anything you desire." He patted the wallet he'd tossed onto the console. "Mr. Cramer is a man of means."

Jenna nudged Gavin. "Time to wake up."

Gavin woke with a start, his lids flying open. Jenna brushed the back of her hand against his cheek. What nightmares had disturbed his sleep? What nightmares lay ahead?

"Are you okay?"

He nodded, his eyes wide. "No snow."

"That's right, but it's still chilly, so we'll put our jackets on when we leave the car."

Cade slung his bag over his body as he exited the car. "Sit tight. I'll check in, and then we'll park."

Less than fifteen minutes later, Jenna was spinning around the sitting room of their suite, her arms out to her sides. "This is heaven. How did you score a suite?"

"It's all they had left. Nobody has checked out yet for the day." He crouched in front of the safe in the closet and waved to Gavin, who had the remote control gripped in one hand and was aiming it at the TV. "Are you ready for some breakfast, Gavin?"

Jenna dropped her arms and scooped up Gavin, remote and all. "He's ready for a bath right now."

"Yeah, I guess the Cramer family better clean up because we don't want to attract any unwanted attention."

Jenna hugged Gavin closer. "How long are we going to stay here?"

"Until we hear back from Prospero and they finish what they hopefully started and set you up in a secure location." Cade walked on his knees from the safe, where he'd stashed most of the contents of his bag, to the mini bar. He held up a candy bar. "Do you want a three-dollar chocolate bar?"

She placed her hand over Gavin's eyes and kneed Cade in the back. "No, but that little bottle of tequila looks inviting."

"You could probably use about five of those after what you went through last night." He rose to his feet and wrapped his arms around both her and Gavin. "It's going to get better."

She closed her eyes and breathed in his masculine scent

from her nose squished against his chest. "Can't get much worse."

She scrubbed a couple of days' dirt and grime from Gavin in the tub. If only she could scrub away his memories as easily. How much of this turmoil would stick with him in the years to come? He'd just seen his second dead body in as many days.

"Any more scrubbing and Gavin's going to turn pink."

Jenna jumped at the sound of Cade's voice and dropped the washcloth into the soapy water. "Do you think all this is going to affect him?"

Cade perched on the edge of the tub and circled his fingers in the water. "You're asking me? I'm no expert on childhood trauma."

"How much of your father's…indiscretions do you recall?"

His hand stilled in the water as the rings continued to expand. "That was different. We never knew what was going on. My father presented a different face to us. I was ten by the time he left, so of course, I remember all the drama surrounding that."

"But it made you a stronger person." She reached around him for Gavin's towel. "Maybe this will do the same for Gavin."

He grabbed the towel, gripping it between them, his knuckles almost as white as the terry cloth. "Gavin will be fine."

She met his dark eyes, blazing with some inner emotion, and for that moment she believed him.

She left a sweet-smelling Gavin with Cade, watching morning cartoons while she took her turn in the shower.

Fifteen minutes later, with her hair wrapped in a towel, she wedged her shoulder against the bathroom door and listened to Gavin try to explain the characters in his favorite cartoon to Cade. Could Cade really be as interested as he sounded?

She rounded the corner and smiled as Cade counted off the names of the superheroes on his fingers.

"Do I have that right?"

"Now the bad guys."

"Oh, I know all the bad guys." He looked up and gave her a grimace. Then he recited the cartoon villains' names as if he'd done battle with them himself.

If only the real villains could be defeated as handily as the ones in Gavin's world.

They decided to stick close to the hotel and have breakfast in the restaurant downstairs. Cade insisted on a table in the back corner and grabbed the seat with his back to a wall, facing the entrance.

Through his smiles and jokes, he still had an edge. Jenna knew he kept his gun close, tucked in the inside pocket of his jacket, which he didn't remove.

The waitress dropped off their check and hovered over their cups with the coffeepot. "Top that off for you?"

"I'll take a little more, thanks." Jenna shoved her cup closer to the edge of the table.

Cade declined and reached for his wallet. He pulled out his phone instead. It buzzed in his hand as he checked the display.

Knots tightened in Jenna's stomach. "Is it Prospero?"

"No, it's my father."

Chapter Ten

Tension crept through every muscle as Cade stared at the display.

Jenna's words flowed from across the table. "Your father? How...why?"

He stabbed the talk button. "Yeah?"

"Son?" Kevin cleared his throat. "It's your old man."

"This is not a good time, Kevin." Cade refused to call the man *father*.

"When is it ever a good time when you're in the spy business, eh?" He coughed his smoker's cough. "But you gave me your private number and told me to call when I was ready to see you."

"Maybe I'm not ready to see you." The lie rolled off Cade's tongue. He'd been the one to initiate contact with Kevin Stark, more for his brother Kyle's sake than his own. But once he'd heard Kevin's voice, heard that infectious chuckle again, the childhood memories had come streaming across his brain. Good memories. Memories of a life lived with a devil-may-care father who'd been the life of every party and every schoolboy's best friend.

Until he'd gone on the lam for embezzling hundreds of thousands of dollars, leaving his family to deal with the fallout.

"I know. I know. I don't blame you, but the truth is, boy, I don't have much longer."

Cade couldn't help the sick feeling that roiled his gut, so he clenched his jaw. "What does that mean?"

"It's these damned cancer sticks." He coughed for effect because the old man was all about the performance. "Never thought they'd get to me, but it turns out I have throat cancer."

Cade's eye twitched. Ironic to think the man with the silver tongue might be silenced. "Sorry to hear it."

"No, you're not." Kevin chuckled, and Cade gripped the phone harder. "Like I said, I don't blame you, but I would like to see my boys once more before I kick the bucket."

"Kyle's still in Chicago."

"I know. I've already spoken to him. Your brother is more forgiving than you." He clicked his tongue. "Not that I blame you."

Cade had been willing to see Kevin when Kyle had located him, but Kevin had had some business to clear up first. Shut down again. Cade had shrugged it off at the time, but his father's rejection, his second rejection, had wounded him. Now his instinct told him to return the favor, but Kevin's chuckle and all it represented lingered between them.

Cade shifted his gaze to Jenna, who spread her hands and raised her brows. "Like I said, not good timing."

"I'm in Vegas, Cade. I'll meet you anywhere. I can be on the next flight to anywhere, unless it's overseas. Then I'm off to Chicago and…who knows how many weeks or days I have left?"

He should just tell the old man he was in Europe. Squeezing his eyes shut, he pinched the bridge of his nose. "Maybe you could see Kyle first and circle through the southwest in a few weeks."

Maybe he'd at least have Jenna and Gavin in a safe location by then. Maybe the person who had the plans would reveal himself by then.

"So you *are* close by."

"Close enough."

"Is my grandson with you?"

Cade almost dropped the phone. "Who told you I had a son?"

"Relax, Cade. Your mother told me before she passed away."

"You never told me you were in touch with Mom."

"A married couple doesn't owe their kids everything. Your mom meant a lot to me. We touched base throughout the years."

Cade flattened a hand against his scalp. Another betrayal. His mother had never told him and Kyle she'd had contact with Kevin. "My son's not with me. I'm on assignment, and it wouldn't be a good idea for me to bring him along, anyway."

"Bring pictures, then. Give me a time and a place, and I'll be there."

Kevin had detected a chink in Cade's armor and had gone for the parry.

"I—I have nothing, son. I want, no I *need* to see you and Kyle before I leave this earth. I need redemption, Cade. Haven't you ever needed redemption?"

And the thrust.

Through half-lidded eyes, Cade watched Gavin draw patterns with the tines of his fork in the syrup left over on his plate.

"I'm near Albuquerque. I'll figure something out and get back to you."

When Cade ended the call, he knew he'd been sucked in again. Maybe this time he could get some closure, or whatever the pop psychologists were calling it these days.

"So, that was your father."

He peeled a couple of bills from his stack and dropped them onto the table. "Yeah."

"Obviously not the first time you've talked to him."

"After Mom died, Kyle insisted I use my resources to track down Kevin." He shrugged. "He wasn't too hard to find, but Kyle was the one who contacted him."

"But you haven't seen him yet?" Jenna whipped Gavin's napkin from his lap and handed it to him. "Wipe your mouth."

"When we first contacted him, he said he had to get some things in order."

"He's in order now?" Her eyes narrowed.

Jenna had been outraged on his behalf when he'd told her the sad story of his father's criminal life and abandonment of his family. Then she'd become fiercely protective of him. He'd detected a lot of irony in that because he was supposed to be the tough guy. But after seeing how Jenna had responded to everything life had thrown at her since, it made perfect sense.

"Kevin's ill—throat cancer."

"That's too bad. Now that he's on death's door, he wants to see you?"

"Something like that."

She sat up in her seat. "You're not taking Gavin to see him, are you?"

"Of course not, but apparently Mom told Kevin about Gavin before she died." He shook his head and took a gulp of water from the half-empty glass in front of him. "I didn't even know Mom had been in touch with the old…guy."

"I thought she hated him almost as much as you hated him?"

"Maybe all that hate's not so good."

She held up her hands. "I'm not judging you for wanting to see him, Cade. It will give you closure."

He laughed and her eyebrows shot up. "I know it's a hackneyed expression, but there's truth in it."

"Don't I know it."

She tapped his phone on the table between them. "Nothing from Prospero yet?"

"Not yet. I got confirmation of the messages I sent earlier, so I'm sure Prospero took care of the situation at the Arizona outpost. Jim is in custody and Miyata is safe."

"Do you think Jim ever met Zendaris?"

"I doubt it. Jim was just another pawn, and that's the danger. Zendaris has them all over."

Jenna's gaze darted from table to table in the restaurant as if expecting to see a Zendaris pawn drinking a cup of coffee. "Do you think it's okay to do some shopping here?"

"We're safe here for now. Zendaris knows I'm with you and he realizes he'll have a harder time getting what he wants." He reached across the table and tweaked Gavin's nose. "In fact, I'm going to stay with you until those plans surface and Zendaris knows I don't have them."

"Really?" Jenna's voice squeaked and she grabbed his hand. "Really?"

"Is that so hard to believe? After what happened at the compound, I decided I couldn't bail on you again."

Her fingernails dug into his flesh. "I wouldn't call it bailing. You have a job to do, and if staying with us takes you away from tracking down Zendaris, I'd rather have you on the job."

"That's a one-eighty from just two days ago when your claws came out at the sight of me."

She rubbed his hand where her nails had left crescent indentations. "I know what's at stake now. Maybe I always knew. When Prospero hired you, I had my chance then to leave you."

"I'm glad you didn't." He threaded his fingers through hers. "Even though we've both paid a high price."

"I don't mind paying the price, but I don't want Gavin to live his life in hiding. Do you think Zendaris will back off when the owner of the plans steps forward?"

"He'll back off, but I don't want to sugarcoat this, Jenna. None of us who were involved in that operation will be safe until Zendaris is—" he glanced at Gavin busily jamming his straw into the lid of his cup "—out of the picture."

"Then you need to make sure he is. So maybe it's not a good idea for you to play bodyguard for me and Gavin."

"There were three others on that team with me. I think they can pick up the slack. Maybe Gage already has his informant." He slapped the table. "Now, let's find some clothes that fit."

They shopped for a few hours, and Cade didn't even mind waiting as Jenna tried on jeans and sweaters. It all had a comfortable married-couple feel to it, which he and Jenna had never had the luxury of experiencing. He liked it.

With their shopping done, they picked up some sandwiches and brought them back to the hotel.

Jenna handed Gavin a small bottle of water and a napkin. "What did you decide to do about your…Kevin?"

"If he can get out here from Vegas, I'll see him tomorrow."

"Here in Albuquerque?"

"No."

"You don't want him to see Gavin?"

"Nobody needs to know where you and Gavin are right now. There are a couple of small towns outside of Albuquerque, and I'll find some watering hole for a meeting place. That's more his style, anyway."

She peeled back the paper on her sandwich. "Give him a chance to apologize. It will be good for both of you."

Cade snorted. "Who says he's going to apologize? He's probably going to hit me up for money."

She stopped fussing with the sandwich and grabbed his wrist. "Are you preparing yourself for that?"

"I'm not expecting much more." Cade jumped to his feet and paced to the window, angry at the lump that formed in his throat. Angry that he couldn't keep an impassive face in front of Jenna.

"It's okay to let that little boy inside of you hope for something more, some kind of connection to the man you clearly adored as a child."

Cade pounded his chest. "There's no little boy in here. He slipped away years ago."

Rolling her eyes, Jenna plucked up half of her sandwich. "Don't be afraid to let him out, Cade. Even if he's disappointed again."

"No need to be disappointed. I told you, I'm not expecting much from Kevin."

"Probably the best way to go." She sighed and took a big bite of her sandwich.

Cade took advantage of her full mouth by changing the subject. "Prospero has been strangely silent. I would've expected someone to contact me by now, at least to tell me what went down with Jim."

Jenna circled her finger in the air while she chewed. "Maybe they don't have a place for me yet."

"For us. I'm not leaving you this time, Jenna. More than any Prospero safe house or relocation plan, I can keep you and Gavin safe."

"You've been doing a great job so far."

"Is that sarcasm?"

She dropped her sandwich. "Absolutely not. I don't

think we would've even made it out of Utah if you hadn't shown up."

"Maybe, but the warehouse and the Prospero outpost didn't work out too great. I put you in even more danger."

"But if we'd never gotten out of Lovett Peak, we never would've…" She brushed some crumbs from her fingertips. "Never mind. We're glad you're here. Aren't we, Gavin?"

Gavin nodded, his cheeks bulging.

Cade had a sudden urge to hold his son, so he sat next to him on the couch and dragged Gavin into his lap, sticky hands and all.

Gavin curled one arm around Cade's neck and fed him a pickle, and that damned lump in Cade's throat got even harder to swallow.

One thing Cade knew for sure—from now on he'd take better care of his family than his father ever did.

THE FOLLOWING DAY, JUST about sunset, Cade kissed the soft cheek of his sleeping son. "Keep the chain on the door at all times, don't open for anyone and don't leave the room for anything—not even to get ice down the hall."

"I'm not going anywhere, but what if the security guard you rented for the evening knocks?"

"Don't even answer for him. I paid him plenty to take some extra swings down this hallway, but my instructions didn't include knocking on your door." Cade pressed his hands against the hermetically sealed window and scanned the outside of the hotel for the hundredth time. Jenna had complained earlier that such an expensive suite didn't even have a balcony or windows that opened, but Cade welcomed the inconvenience.

Nobody could scale this building and get in through the window.

"There's a gun in the safe if you need it."

"You already told me that." She bounded from the bed and wrapped her arms around him from behind. "We're going to be fine. Go see your father. It might be your last chance."

Cade had struggled with the decision of whether to go through with his meeting with Kevin, but Jenna had pointed out that once Prospero relocated them, Cade might not have another chance to see his father.

He threaded his fingers through hers and kissed her hand. "I left the phone number and address of the bar by the telephone. Use the hotel phone to call, not your own cell."

Moving to his side, she saluted. "Got it. Now you'd better get going."

He pulled her back into his arms and wedged a finger beneath her chin. "I love you. Never stopped."

"I never stopped, either, not even when I hated you."

He ran the tip of his tongue along the seam of her lips, and then sealed his mouth over hers. She melted against him, her body warm and pliant.

She pulled away first because he wasn't capable. They touched foreheads, their breathing shallow and erratic.

"We're going to start over, Cade. I won't even say we'll begin again when this is over because it may never be over. It doesn't matter. We're going to have a life together, aren't we?"

"I'm going to do everything in my power to make that happen. Last time…"

She placed a finger over his lips. "Last time doesn't matter, either, only the future."

He kissed her again and grabbed his jacket. "You've got a gun. Don't be afraid to use it."

He stood outside the hotel door until he heard the chain slide into place. Then he tracked down the security guard he'd hired for the night to let him know he was leaving.

Cade headed west on the I-40. Before calling Kevin to set up this meeting, he asked the hotel staff to recommend a place on the outskirts of the city where a man could get a drink and have a conversation.

He didn't know what to expect from his reunion with Kevin, but he didn't want the awkwardness of someplace too quiet and formal or a rowdy club scene. The sports bar the concierge recommended seemed like the perfect spot. Kevin insisted he'd have no trouble getting there by eight o'clock that night.

Cade would've preferred to meet during daytime, but Kevin couldn't make it out any earlier and Cade and Jenna might be on their way to parts unknown tomorrow.

The traffic thinned out the farther he got from Albuquerque's city center. He glanced at his cell phone in the cup holder. Nothing from Jenna, although he'd been gone just twenty-five minutes. And nothing from Prospero. Why the silence on that end? Nobody had even called him to give him news about Jim—the whys and whens of his betrayal.

He shoved his foot against the accelerator. People turned traitor for lots of reasons—ideological, love and money— always money.

A neon rattlesnake curled around a lighted sign that read Ted's Sports Bar, although what a snake had to do with sports, Cade didn't have a clue. Maybe it was a holdover from the previous bar to inhabit this lonely stretch of road.

Cade cruised into the busy parking lot, swiveling his head from side to side. Trucks, motorcycles, minivans and the occasional luxury sedan hinted at an eclectic clientele.

Would he recognize Kevin after all these years?

He parked and strolled through the door of the bar, his new boots scuffing the wood floor. Jenna hadn't been the only one shopping yesterday. Cade figured he'd pick up a pair of boots to fit into this southwestern town, but he passed on the cowboy hat.

Two flat-screen TVs blared with the same basketball game, barely competing with the loud voices and laughter that cascaded through the room. How exactly was this atmosphere conducive to conversation? At least all the activity would drown out any awkward silences between him and Kevin.

Cade's gaze traveled around the room, flitting over clutches of people drinking and socializing, focusing in on old, solitary, sick-looking men.

Then he heard the chuckle above the cacophony. Unmistakable. He jerked his head in its general direction and he was pretty sure his eyes were bugging out of their sockets when he spied Kevin.

The old, solitary man he'd been seeking had a seat at the bar, right in the thick of things. A small band of men and women gathered around the long, lean raconteur, laughing and hanging on his every word.

His thick, silver hair brushed back from his high forehead gleamed in the bright light of the bar. His white teeth stood out from his tanned skin, the lines etching an interesting pattern on his rugged, still-handsome face.

As if sensing the scrutiny, Kevin spun around on his barstool and he narrowed his blue eyes. He turned back to his companions, slapped some money on the bar, shook some hands and kissed some cheeks.

He sauntered toward Cade, drink in hand and flashy alligator boots on his feet. He didn't look like a man suffering from throat cancer or any other kind of cancer.

Kevin thrust out his hand. "Well, look at you, all grown up and looking just like your old man, even though you always had your mother's eyes."

Cade flinched and Kevin cracked a smile.

"Okay, you're taller. Kyle look like you?"

"Kyle…" Was this the conversation you had with a father you hadn't seen in almost twenty years? Cade's tongue refused to form any recognizable syllables.

"Nah, you got your mother's coloring and Kyle got her looks." Kevin grabbed his arm. "Let's grab that booth in the corner."

Cade slid onto the red banquette across from Kevin and licked his lips. He had to start acting like a grown-up, not a tongue-tied kid.

"Sweetheart—" Kevin waved to a cocktail waitress in shorts and a tight T-shirt "—can you bring us a pitcher of beer? Whatever's good on tap."

"You got it, Kev."

"Kev? How long have you been here?"

"I made good time from Vegas. I've been hanging out a few hours."

"A few hours?" Knots tightened in Cade's gut. "You could've called me and I would've met you earlier."

"Truth is—" Kevin tapped the side of his glass "—I had to screw up my courage."

This time, Cade laughed, a laugh that loosened the tightness of his jaw and the stiffness of his neck. "That'll be the day."

"I'm dead serious, boy. It's not easy for me to come crawling back to my sons to beg a little forgiveness."

Cade leaned back in the booth, crossing his arms. "I haven't heard any begging…or anything about forgiveness."

"Here you go, hon." The waitress placed a pitcher on the table between father and son and then clinked down a couple of frosted beer mugs.

"Thanks, sweetheart." Kevin tucked a few bills into the waistband of the woman's short shorts and patted her hip.

She batted her eyelashes and slapped his hand. "Watch those roving hands, Kev."

"I'd like to watch them rove all over your pretty backside."

The waitress rolled her eyes and clicked her tongue. "You old devil."

She sashayed away, and Cade shook his head. "You ever hear of sexual harassment? You can't treat women like that."

Kevin smacked the table. "Did you see her complaining? Besides, I'll let you in on a little secret." He looked both ways as if expecting someone to be listening in. "Gray hair excuses a lot of bad behavior."

"You indulged in bad behavior long before you had gray hair."

"Yeah, I did. I admit it." He poured the golden liquid into the two mugs and raised his. "To a life of bad behavior."

Cade didn't bring his glass to meet Kevin's, but he didn't have to. Kevin touched his mug to Cade's and slurped his beer through the foam.

Cade pulled his cell phone from his pocket and glanced at the blank display. What the hell was he doing here? He should be back at the hotel with his wife and son. If he'd thought meeting Kevin would offer any kind of resolution for him, he'd been dreaming.

The man hadn't changed one bit. In fact, this lecherous side of Kevin, which Cade had been too young to notice before, made him sink even lower in Cade's estimation. He'd have to warn Kyle.

The question remained—why had the old man contacted him now? He'd made it clear last year he had no interest in a family reunion.

Cade cleared his throat and took a sip of beer, the malty flavor filling his mouth. "You're not dying, are you?"

Kevin raised a brow and one side of his mouth. "We're all dying from the day we're born."

Cade ground his teeth together. "Your death is not imminent."

"It could be."

"Cut to the chase, Kevin. Why did you want to see me? Why now?"

"I'm broke." He raised his mug to his lips, watching Cade over the rim with his faded blue eyes.

Cade's skin prickled with anger, the warm flush threatening to creep up his neck and suffuse his face. "You've come to the wrong place, and don't try to hit up Kyle. He takes on more pro bono work than paying clients in that law practice of his."

"The way I see it, you're a virtual gold mine."

"You've got the wrong Navy SEAL." Cade held up his hands before taking a gulp of beer to put out the fire in his belly.

"Don't hand me that bull. You're not a Navy SEAL anymore."

Cade clenched the handle of his mug, feeling as if he could break it clean off.

"And I know for a fact you're married to a girl who's rolling in dough. Oil money, right?"

Cade's eye twitched. How had Kevin found out so much about him? Mom? "That's my wife's family. My wife has no money."

"When the parents have wealth like that, it eventually trickles down to the kids."

"My wife is estranged from her family. Even if she did have access to her parents' money, what makes you think I'd hand it over to you?"

"Come on, Cade. You're talking to an old grifter here." He folded his hands around his mug looking almost pious.

"I know all kinds of ways to make people part with their money."

"This meeting is over." Cade hunched into his jacket and yanked some bills from his pocket.

Kevin's eyes narrowed to slits. "Get me some money, Cade."

The man had lost his grip on reality. Cade crumpled the money in his fist and threw it in Kevin's face. "Here's your money. The only money you'll ever see from me or my wife."

Kevin plucked up the bills and flattened them on the table, running his thumb across the creases. When he looked up again, the customary smile had replaced the hard lines.

"Get me your wife's money, Cade." He took an almost delicate sip from his mug. "Or I'll lead them straight to your son."

Chapter Eleven

Cade slid his weapon from his inside pocket, swung it beneath the table and released the safety with a click. "Tell me what you told them right now or you'll never be able to father another sorry SOB as long as you live."

The lazy smile froze on Kevin's lips. His faded blue eyes darted around the bar.

"Looking for support? Hoping to muster a defense from those fair-weather friends at the bar? Or maybe the waitress you disrespected will help out? Don't you get it, Kevin? The people you charm and con aren't real friends. You don't have the depth or loyalty to have a real friend...or a family."

Kevin wiped a trickle of sweat from his brow with the back of his hand and chugged the rest of his beer. "Just so you know, I didn't contact them. They contacted me."

"That's not saying much, Kev. How would you know to contact them, anyway?" Cade rested the gun on his knee. "How did they get in touch with you, and what kind of offer did they make you?"

"They called me out of the blue last month. Said you had something they wanted, and they'd be willing to pay big bucks if I could get my hands on your kid and turn him over."

Cade tightened his jaw. "You never talked to Mom before she died about me, my son or anything else, did you?

You found out about my son from a bunch of international thugs."

"That's what I told them, boy." He hunched forward, almost tipping over his empty mug. "I said I didn't even know you had a son, so there was no way you were going to let me get anywhere near him."

"Did they believe you?"

"I think so. They didn't contact me again, although I think they followed me for a bit. I can tell when I'm being shadowed."

"Maybe it was the FBI tailing you again."

"Those boys got nothing on me." Kevin winked. "So where's my thanks? I told them to get lost."

"Only because you spoke the truth. You knew I'd never let you within a hundred miles of my son."

"We can do this together, Cade."

The man couldn't sink any lower in his estimation. "You really expect me to help you turn my son over to an arms dealer who has the worst intentions toward our country?"

Kevin tapped his head. "I've got it all figured out. If that rich bitch you're married to won't give you any dough, this can work out for you, too."

Did he just call Jenna a *rich bitch?* He should shoot him now and be done with it.

"Let me take your boy, and I'll hand him over and get my money. You give them whatever it is they want in exchange for your son, and then I'll split the cash with you." He poured himself another beer, which foamed over the side and puddled on the table. "Doesn't that sound like a good plan?"

Cade's lips twisted into a smile. "You're really a dumb SOB, aren't you? Do you really believe these people will let my son live? Wait, wait. I know you don't care about that, but do you really think they'll let *you* live?"

Kevin's face paled beneath his tan, and the lines on his face deepened.

"These people aren't like some hick in Vegas you can fleece out of his first jackpot." He gripped Kevin's wrist in a vise. "Where are they now? Do they know you're meeting with me here?"

Kevin jerked his arm but couldn't break free of Cade's grip. "I told you. I blew them off. This is my scheme."

"It's not a very bright one. Did you really think I'd turn over my son for money?"

"You abandoned him once, didn't you?"

A cold anger crept over Cade's flesh. He threw Kevin's arm back at him and slid from the booth, pocketing his weapon. "Not for money."

Kevin rubbed his wrist. "Whatever you tell yourself to get through the night, boy."

Cade leveled a finger at the man he'd never call father. "If you come near me or my family again, and that includes Kyle, I'll kill you."

He spun on his heel and stalked out of the bar just as a cheer went up for the basketball game.

When Cade got into the car, he slumped in the front seat and dug his cell phone from his pocket. He called the hotel room and Jenna answered on the first ring.

"Is everything okay there?"

"Everything's fine. Gavin is still out, and I'm watching a movie. I-it's still early. Is everything okay there?"

"I'm on my way home." He'd already decided not to tell Jenna about Kevin's betrayal. Why add to her worries?

"It didn't go well, did it? I can tell by your voice."

"Once a scumbag, always a scumbag. I don't know why I thought it would be any different."

"Because he's your father and you wanted to salvage something of that relationship."

He put his cell on speaker and wheeled out of the parking lot. "There's nothing to salvage there."

"That bad, huh?"

Worse. So much worse. "Yeah, that bad."

"Is he really dying?"

"As he put it, we're all dying from the day we're born."

"Seriously? What did he want from you?"

"Money."

"Oh, Cade, I'm so sorry."

"I'm not. Seeing him for what he really is freed me. I don't have to wonder anymore."

She sucked in a breath over the phone. "I can hear it in your voice—closure. Hurry back."

"Why?" He'd blurted out the word in a sharper tone than he'd intended. What if Kevin had been lying? What if he'd told Zendaris's men about their meeting?

Jenna paused. Then her low voice poured into his ear like sweet honey. "Because I'm your wife, and we haven't been together for three long years."

His anxiety morphed into desire in a second, and he let the car have its way on the highway. "I'll be right there."

He'd already made sure no one followed him out of the bar's parking lot. His lead foot got him back to the hotel in less time than it had taken him to get to that sports bar. He met the security guard doing another round on their hallway.

"No trouble tonight?"

"Everything went just fine, sir, and management never noticed I was spending most of my time on the ninth floor."

Cade slipped the man another bill. "Thanks."

He tapped on the door, and several seconds later Jenna opened it against the chain. "Just want to make sure what I'm seeing out of the peephole is the real thing."

He spread his arms. "I'm for real."

She shut the door, and the chain scraped. This time when she opened the door, he stepped through, slamming it behind him. With one hand, he reengaged the chain, and with his other arm he swept Jenna against his chest.

She wrapped her arms around his waist and he buried his face in the honeyed strands of her hair. He should've never left her for Kevin, for some illusion of a father who didn't exist, who'd never existed.

Turning her face to his, she cupped his jaw with one hand. "Are you okay?"

"I have you and Gavin. That's all I need."

She stood on her tiptoes, her body leaning against his, and kissed his mouth. With her lips forming the words against his, she whispered, "I need you, too."

"Gavin?" He peered over her shoulder into the hotel room lit with the TV's blue flickering light.

"He's sleeping. I put him in the bedroom."

Cade swept her up in his arms and carried her toward the bed. Clasping her to his chest, he kissed her and once again felt like a drowning man. He never wanted to come up for air.

She kicked her legs. "Put me down. As much as I want to make love with you right now, I'm not going to do it standing up. I've waited too long to be satisfied with a quickie."

He snorted. "A quickie? I hope you had a nice rest while I was gone because I'm going to spend all night reacquainting myself with every inch of your hot body."

He dropped her onto the bed, and her cotton nightshirt hiked up her silky thighs. At least they looked silky. He perched on the edge of the bed beside her and ran his hands up her legs as she shivered beneath his touch. Definitely silky.

She reached up and her fingers fumbled with the zipper

on his jacket. "Why are you still wearing this? Why are you still wearing anything at all?"

When his jacket gaped open, he yanked it off and tossed it toward the chair. He missed.

She sat up, her knees wedging against his thigh, and began unbuttoning his denim shirt. She grabbed the material in her fists and brought it to her face. "You smell like booze."

"The hazards of hanging out in bars. I can fix that." He shrugged out of his shirt and sent it the way of his jacket.

"How many layers do you have on?" She plucked at his T-shirt.

"A lot more than you." He gripped the ends of her nightshirt and yanked it over her head.

Goose bumps raced across her creamy skin and he chafed her upper arms. "Now you're cold. Get under the covers."

"Not without you." She tugged at his T-shirt, and he pulled it off.

He pulled of his boots and dropped them to the floor. Then he slipped out of his jeans, taking his boxers and socks with them.

Jenna's gaze traveled over his naked body, heating his flesh, making him hard.

She tilted her head to the side, and her blond hair fell over one eye. "Everything looks pretty much as I remember, but I'm going to have to do a closer inspection to make sure."

He stretched out on the bed next to her, his feet hanging off the end. "I'm all yours."

She straddled him and began a long journey down the length of his body. Her fingertips traced his grooves and the hard lines of his muscles. Her tongue followed, licking and tasting and driving him wild with impatience.

When she skimmed her fingernails up the insides of his thighs, he'd had enough. He encircled her waist and flipped her onto her back, taking the upper hand.

She widened her eyes, a wicked smile claiming her full lips. "I thought you were enjoying that."

"A little too much."

"Is that possible?"

He pinned her hands above her head. "Do you want to find out?"

He kissed her lips and the sweetness he found there blotted out the bitter taste from Kevin's words. He trailed his tongue to her throat, stopping at the base. When he pressed his lips against her beating pulse, he felt warmth and life. It soaked into his skin, giving him sustenance.

He cupped her breasts, fuller since the birth of their son, and buried his face in their fragrant warmth.

She dug her nails into his buttocks. "If you're going to take a half hour on every body part, I can see why this is going to take us all night."

He nipped at her nipple and she squeaked. "I've waited long enough. If I want to take a half hour with each of your delicious body parts, I will."

"Okay. Wake me up when you're done with the inventory." She wrapped her legs around his thighs, crossing her arms behind her head.

Heat crept up his neck. For their first time together, Jenna didn't need a man interested in slow, healing love. She needed a man who knew how to take care of business. The healing part could come later.

"You think my efforts are going to put you to sleep, huh?" He hooked his arms beneath her knees and hoisted her legs over his shoulders.

Then he dragged his tongue down the length of her body.

When he dipped below her navel, he brushed her warm folds back with his thumbs.

She shuddered and arched her back, positioning herself inches from his mouth. He blew on her moist flesh while he rotated his thumbs.

She gasped and lifted her head, pressing her chin to her chest. "You're not going to take a half hour down there, are you?"

He dipped one finger inside her. "I just might."

Groaning, she flopped back against the pillow. With his finger still inserted in her tight walls, he nibbled around her edges, his tongue darting out for small tastes of her honey.

Then he went to work in earnest, and she didn't stand a chance against his tender assault. He brought her to climax within minutes, and as she began to come down from her high, shaking and moaning, he thrust his tongue inside her again and again.

She clutched at his hair, her fingernails digging into his scalp. Her thighs clamped around his head, drowning him in her musky scent.

He sucked her into his mouth, as gently as a soft, ocean breeze. Must've felt like a gale force wind because she screamed as he toyed with her, drawing her closer to the edge of the precipice.

This time he left her hanging. As he straddled her body, she squirmed beneath him, her hands clawing at his chest for release. He nudged her thighs apart and drove into her, lifting her bottom from the bed. He pulled out and thrust again, and she shattered beneath him.

Her climax clutched around him as he pounded against her. She lay spent for a moment and he slowed his movement. Then she reached up and held his face in her hands. Her blue gaze never leaving his, she whispered. "Your turn."

"Don't worry. I plan to take it." He pulled out and flipped her over while she dragged a pillow beneath her chest and lifted her hips in blatant invitation.

He rose to his knees and steadied her with his hands on either side of her rounded bottom. He rode her from behind, his skin slapping hers in an erotic rhythm that signaled their ultimate connection.

When he came, he couldn't stifle the growls born from his primal satisfaction. He also couldn't let go of his wife. Still shuddering with his release, he reached around and stroked her where their bodies met. She shivered and pushed against his probing fingers.

Her heat grew around him once again. Her creamy derriere undulated against his belly, and he hardened in response. This time she climaxed with a whimper instead of a cry. A long, soft sigh escaped her lips, and her body melted beneath his, trapping his hand between her hot flesh and the mattress below.

He slipped out of her and rolled to the side.

She opened one eye. "I can't move."

"That opens up all kinds of possibilities." He traced the beads of her spine with the tip of his finger, lightly following her bottom crease. He tucked his fingers between her legs and stroked her damp inner thighs.

"Mmm." She burrowed her face into the pillow, inching her legs apart.

He rubbed her bottom with the flat of his hand, while the fingers of his other hand swirled closer to her heated core. "Do you want another?"

She shifted her head to the side, a guilty smile playing across her lips. "I wouldn't mind, but—" she ran her hand down his belly and stroked him "—you're not ready yet."

"*Yet* is the operative word." He nudged one finger inside while he pinched her flesh with the others.

She sucked in a breath and jerked at his touch. "You do have magic fingers."

"Don't forget my magic tongue."

"And your magic…"

Without ever releasing his hold on her, he nudged her onto her back and continued his magic.

CADE HAD FALLEN INTO a drugged sleep, which someone was trying to spoil. The reality of making love to Jenna and his dreams had merged into one long night of pleasure and satiation.

He'd held her close all night, their limbs tangled, their hands always searching, their lips meeting in hot, hungry kisses. He didn't know where his body left off and hers began.

He reached for her again, his fingers crawling across cool, empty sheets. Empty.

He struggled against the weights on his eyelids as someone poked him in the side. "Cade, Cade, wake up. Isn't that the bar where you met your father last night?"

Jenna's words acted like a splash of cold water on his face. He rubbed his eyes, kicking the tangled sheets from his naked body. "What?"

"On the TV. Wait. I think I can pause this and rewind."

Cade pushed up to a sitting position, swinging his legs over the side of the bed. Why would Ted's Sports Bar be on TV? He blinked and squinted at the neon snake frozen on the screen, emergency vehicles parked in front of the bar.

"What the hell is going on? What's this story?"

She kept the remote pointed at the TV as she twisted her body toward him. "Th-there's been a murder."

Cade felt as if he was falling and he grabbed the sheets in his fists. Wait. It could be anyone. It was a bar.

"Can you play it back?"

She fumbled with the remote until the figures on the TV sped in reverse. Then she stabbed another button and the morning news anchors changed their demeanors from happy to serious.

"In other news, a man's body was found in the alley behind Ted's Sports Bar in the early morning hours when one of the employees went out to dump the trash. Colleen Temple is on the scene. Colleen, has the man been identified?"

Colleen adjusted a strand of hair and arranged her face into a frown. "Pat, the man, in his early sixties, has been identified from his driver's license, but police are waiting to contact his next of kin. One bar patron, who was here last night, is claiming the man's alligator boots were stolen. A charge the police will neither confirm nor deny."

Cade's gut rolled and he yanked the sheet, ripping it in half.

"Cade?"

"It's Kevin. They murdered him and we have to get out of here."

Chapter Twelve

Jenna's knees buckled and she dropped to the bed. Had Cade lost his mind? What did Kevin Stark have to do with Nico Zendaris?

"How do you know it's Kevin? Th-there could've been plenty of sixty-year-old men at the bar last night."

"The alligator boots, Jenna. The murdered man had alligator boots and so did Kevin."

"Still, there could be lots of older men wearing alligator boots in New Mexico."

His dark eyes drilled her. "Really?"

"Why would Zendaris kill your...Kevin?"

"I can give you plenty of motives. I should've gotten you and Gavin out of here last night. What reason did he give me to trust one word out of his mouth?"

Cade's naked form, his muscles hard and ready, looked untouchable. His tight jaw and blazing eyes made him look unreachable.

"I don't understand, Cade."

"Get Gavin ready. I don't have time to explain."

And just like that, the husband she'd reclaimed in body and soul last night had hardened into this stranger, giving orders and keeping her in the dark.

This stranger had kept her and Gavin safe, so she followed those orders.

She pulled the hotel terry-cloth robe over her nakedness and stumbled into the adjoining bedroom. Gavin had had his bath last night, so she could get him ready to go in minutes. But why did she have to?

Cade directed tight smiles at Gavin and perfunctory pats on the head, and Gavin picked up on his tension. Then he reacted by refusing to put on his jacket and kicking his mittens across the floor.

Jenna cracked. "You pick those up right now."

Cade parked the new suitcase stuffed with their new clothes in the corner of the room and crouched before Gavin. The lines that worry had carved in his face the past hour softened. "Why did you do that, Gavin?"

"I wanna stay."

"In this place? I've got a better place, and we'll stop at a ghost town on the way. Do you want to go to an Old West ghost town?"

His eyes wide, Gavin nodded. "Are ghosts there?"

"Just a couple of small ones." Cade pointed to the scattered mittens. "Now pick those up like your mother asked you."

Gavin galloped across the floor, scooped up the mittens and shoved them in his pockets.

Jenna blew out a breath. One small crisis averted. If only Zendaris could be distracted by ghost towns.

"That's better. Pancakes or eggs this morning?"

"Both!"

As she slid into the car next to Cade, she touched his arm. "Thanks for defusing that back there. That could've wound up in a major tantrum, and you do not want to see a three-year-old boy throw a tantrum."

"It's not pretty when someone else's kid does it, so I can't imagine it would look any better on my son."

Jenna glanced over her shoulder. Had Gavin noticed

Cade calling him his son? They needed a quiet moment to tell him together, but when exactly would that be?

Cade needed to tell her why Kevin had been murdered and what it had to do with Zendaris and why it prompted them to flee from the most comfortable bed she'd had in three days. The most comfortable bed she'd had in three years, because Cade was beside her.

As Cade pulled out of the hotel parking lot, Jenna closed her eyes and got lost in the sensations of last night. Cade hadn't forgotten what she liked and how she liked it. She always did purr beneath his skilled touch, and nothing had changed.

Jenna gave her cheek a small slap. She had to get her head out of the clouds and her mind out of the bed. Her gaze ticked down to the speedometer as they hit the highway. They were on the run again, which meant danger had descended. So much for the brief respite at the hotel.

"Are you falling asleep over there?"

"Nope. Wide awake."

He lifted one eyebrow. "I could've sworn I saw you slapping yourself."

"I need some coffee…and some information."

"The coffee I can promise you in another half hour or so. The information—" he jerked his thumb at Gavin kicking his feet in the air "—will have to wait."

If Cade couldn't talk about Kevin in veiled references in front of Gavin, it must be bad.

They approached a suburb of Albuquerque and pulled into the parking lot of a chain restaurant. They spent the time at breakfast entertaining Gavin.

Jenna studied Cade coloring his fifth cow. It felt good to share the guilt of uprooting Gavin every fifteen minutes with someone else. Her shoulders ached from all the remorse.

"Where are we headed after this, Cade?" She tried to keep the weariness from her voice.

"We'll go east until I hear from Prospero."

"Why haven't you heard from them yet?"

He shrugged. "Maybe they don't have anything to report, or any help to give."

"We don't need them. Between the two of us and our vast experience, I think we can find a safe place to hole up."

"It would be easier to do with help from Prospero." He scratched his chin with the red crayon, leaving a mark. "They can provide fake IDs, cash, oversight."

"From what I saw in your little black bag, you have IDs, I still have lots of cash and we can provide our own oversight."

"We won't wait for them, but I'm not going to refuse their help when it's offered. If it's offered." His dark eyes clouded over, turning a shade of gray.

It's the first time he'd acknowledged all might not be well with Prospero. Had Jim the traitor been right? Did members of Prospero suspect Cade of having the plans in his possession? Not Cade's team members and not Jack Coburn. Coburn had handpicked Prospero Team Three's members and shared a tight bond with them. And Jack Coburn *was* Prospero.

They finished breakfast and made a beeline for the car. Jenna buckled Gavin into his car seat and draped a blanket across his knees. He usually fell asleep in the car, anyway, but she wanted to make sure he was warm and cozy to speed things along.

The tension between her and Cade was as thick as an early summer fog rolling in from Coronado Bay. Amazing to think that less than twelve hours ago, they'd been wrapped in each other's arms with no boundaries between them.

After about the hundredth time peeking into the backseat, she squeezed the toe of Gavin's boot. "Are you sleeping?"

His long dark lashes fluttered once on his smooth cheeks, but other than that he didn't stir at her touch.

Swinging around to face Cade, she said, "Okay, spill. What the hell happened to Kevin and how do you know Zendaris is responsible?"

His gaze darted to the rearview mirror. "You don't waste any time, do you?"

"I've been cooling my jets for about three hours now. I don't like being kept in the dark."

"You'd rather I blurt all this stuff out in front of Gavin? Isn't that how you kept him feeling secure all these years? You never let the turmoil of your life bubble over in front of him?"

"Yes, but now he's sleeping, so stop stalling."

Cade set his jaw and drilled the highway with his gaze. "When I met with Kevin last night he had a proposition for me."

"A proposition?" Her stomach dipped and did backflips.

"Zendaris had tracked him down somehow." He waited for her gasp to subside. "I guess even Zendaris knew enough that I wouldn't give in to blackmail over my old man if they snatched him."

"How did they find him?"

"I have no idea. How did they find you?" He lifted his shoulders. "They have their resources just like we do."

"What did they want with him?" She held her breath hoping for a different answer than the one she knew in her heart.

"They wanted to use him to get to me. They promised him money if could turn Gavin over to them."

"B-but he refused." Jenna hugged herself because she couldn't hug Cade.

"Did he?" He swerved sharply to avoid roadkill in their lane. "He knew I'd never let him get close to Gavin, so Kevin had another proposition for me."

He stopped speaking and clenched his jaw so tightly that Jenna could hear his teeth grinding.

She waited, afraid to touch him—afraid not to.

After a few minutes, he continued. "Kevin figured we could make a deal with Zendaris. I'd hand Gavin over to Kevin, Kevin would hand Gavin over to Zendaris and then I'd hand the plans over to Zendaris and get Gavin back."

Her jaw dropped. "Kevin really believed that would work? He really believed you'd let your son anywhere near that maniac? Either of those maniacs?"

"I don't know what he believed. The dollar signs had clouded his vision and probably his senses."

"And that's when you left?" She shifted her gaze to her hands folded in her lap, her knuckles white, her fingers red.

Cade sucked in a breath. "Do you think I had something to do with Kevin's murder?"

Did she? When Cade got that dangerous look in his eye, when his muscles coiled into a spring until he looked ready to strike anyone, she didn't know him anymore. That wasn't the same man who could color balloons and cows with Gavin. That wasn't the same man who could tease her to heights of passion.

"No, but I wouldn't blame you if you did."

He drew his brows over his nose and shot a curious look at her. "I didn't. I left."

"What did Kevin tell you about how he left things with Zendaris?"

"He said he'd told them I wouldn't let him anywhere near my son, and didn't know where I was, anyway."

"Either he was lying to you or Zendaris's men thought he was lying to them." She shivered and cranked up the heat. "What if they had tracked Kevin to the bar while he met with you?"

"They may have."

"Kevin called you on your cell phone. What if they have that phone now?" Her gaze darted to the black phone in the cup holder. "What if they call you?"

"I've told you. The phone is special, untraceable. Even when someone calls me, the number doesn't show up on their phone. They're not interested in *calling* me. They'd rather do other things."

"And yet they didn't make a move on you last night?"

"They may have tried." He shoved his foot against the accelerator. "I might have been careless last night, but I always make sure there's nobody following me—always."

"Nobody followed you back to the hotel last night?"

"I made sure of it, but they must've been at the bar. If not when I was at Ted's, then later to meet with Kevin. Who knows? Maybe Kevin had set up a meeting with them, thinking he could make the deal with me and then let them know he'd be getting his hands on Gavin."

"Instead, they killed him."

"I warned him." Cade pinched the bridge of his nose. "I can see him trying to con a couple of thugs for an international arms dealer. He probably thought he had them up to the second they took his life."

His armor seemed to have slipped a little, so she rubbed her knuckles on the rough denim covering his thighs. "I'm sorry, Cade."

"Why?"

"He was your father. You loved him once as a child."

"He wasn't worthy of it."

She turned her head, blowing out a breath and fogging the window. "At that moment he was. At the moment he made you laugh, at the moment he cheered you on at your first swim meet, at the moment he read you a story. He was worthy then."

She didn't know if she was getting through to him at all, but her words made her own nose tingle. She'd never even had those moments with her parents. They'd been too busy with their social scene, taking exotic vacations without her and her sister, using them as props for the obligatory family portrait.

"I want to be there for the long haul with Gavin."

Wiping her cheek, she faced him, or at least his hard profile. "You will be."

"Haven't done such a great job of it yet."

"When are we going to tell him you're his father?"

"Maybe we should wait."

"Really? Wait for what?" In her bones, she felt that Cade needed his son now, needed that connection.

"Maybe we should wait for all this to settle down."

She chewed her lip and clasped her hands between her knees. "Do you want to make sure you can be his father in more than name only?"

"Something like that."

She laughed, and he jerked his head toward her. "Do you want to take that fatherhood class first? Buy a few *dad* clothes? Prepare for fireside chats?"

His forehead creased. "Something wrong with that?"

"Ask any parent—there's not much preparation you can do. You're his father, Cade, and it's high time he knows it."

She folded her arms. "Unless you're scared."

He snorted. "I'm not afraid."

She slid a glance at his hands gripping the steering wheel. "Not even an owner's manual for children would've changed Kevin. He did the best he could, but ultimately he had skewed priorities."

His eyes darted to the rearview mirror. "Yeah, priorities."

By late afternoon, they'd put a few hundred miles between themselves and Kevin's killers. Had Zendaris's men even known Cade was in Albuquerque? Maybe that's why they murdered Kevin. Maybe in the end Kevin wouldn't give them any information about his son and grandson.

Of course, Cade had never thought of that. It wouldn't occur to him now that he was busy distancing himself from his father and the hope of some sort of reconciliation.

They pulled into a small town somewhere near the Colorado border. How could anyone find them here? Of course, she'd never believed she'd be discovered in Lovett Peak.

"How does that look?" Cade pointed a finger over the steering wheel, at a cozy roadside motel.

"Looks like Mr. Cramer may not even have to use his credit card for this place. They're probably just as happy to accept cash."

"Are you implying it's a dump?"

"If it has a shower, a bed and some food nearby, it's heaven."

"Are we home now, Mommy?"

Jenna reached into the backseat and squeezed one of Gavin's bouncing knees. "We're on our way to a new home, honey bunny."

"With him?" He reached out both hands toward Cade and wiggled his fingers.

"We're going to talk about that." Jenna winked. Gavin's comment was the perfect opening.

Cade squealed to a stop next to the motel office. "But now we're going to check into our motel."

Jenna shot Cade a look through narrowed eyes. *Dodged that one.* Cade had been all in her face a few days ago about giving Gavin the big news. Funny how confronting your past could change things.

Cade registered at the front desk and dangled the key from his finger as he led the way outside. "Number fifteen, garden view."

"Do we need to move the car?"

"There's no parking on that side. The woman at the front desk said we're good here."

Their room faced a small courtyard with shrubbery, potted plants and hanging baskets of flowers.

She sniffed the air for their fragrance. "This isn't half bad."

"Not as nice as that suite in Albuquerque."

"Eh, suites are overrated."

He reached past her to push open the door and brushed her arm. "I'll never forget that suite."

She met his dark gaze and knew he wasn't talking about the flat-screen TV. She wanted to kiss him right then and there, kiss away his pain, his disappointment and his fear that he'd be the same kind of dad that Kevin was to him.

But Gavin had scampered into the room ahead of them, and she didn't want to confuse him with any displays of affection toward Cade until they'd had a chance to talk to him.

Gavin had never seen her with a man. Even though she hadn't been with Cade in three years, she'd taken her marriage vows seriously. Heck, no man could compare to Cade, anyway. It had been love at first sight on her end. She'd never believed in that before, but she'd lived it.

Gavin darted around the room and said, "Where's the little bar?"

Cade laughed. "The little bar?"

"He means the minibar, don't you, Gavin?" She dug her fists into her hips. "Looks like someone else will never forget that suite. You've corrupted him with a five-dollar chocolate bar."

"Doesn't look like there are any minibars in here." Cade scooped up Gavin and hoisted him in the air. "But I saw a park on the way, and I'll bet you could use some exercise."

"Ball?" Gavin's brown eyes sparkled and he kicked his feet.

"Sure, we can get a ball. Do you know how to swim?"

"Swimming pool!"

Cade looked at Jenna over the top of Gavin's head. "Does he?"

"He took some lessons at the YMCA in Lovett Peak. I wouldn't say he can swim, but he does a mean dog paddle and he's not afraid of the water at all."

"I wouldn't expect him to be."

"You teach me?" Gavin was patting Cade on top of the head.

"Cade's a great swimmer." Jenna didn't want to waste another minute or refer to Gavin's dad as Cade one more time. She sat on the edge of the bed, and patted the mattress. "Let's sit down for a talk before we run off looking for balls and parks and swimming pools."

Cade's Adam's apple bobbed as he met her eyes, but he took a seat next to her, pulling Gavin into his lap.

Jenna wedged her finger beneath Gavin's chin, turning his head so she could look into his eyes. "Do you remember when you asked me about your daddy?"

He nodded. "'Cuz Sam has a daddy."

"Everyone has a daddy, and so do you. Remember I told you he was away?"

"Uh-huh."

"Well, he's back." She curled her fingers around Gavin's. "Cade is your daddy."

His eyes wide, Gavin tipped his head back to look at

Cade, his gaze searching his father's face. A slow smile curved Gavin's lips. "I have a daddy, too."

Jenna blinked back her tears. "Yes, you do, and he loves you very much."

Cade cleared his throat. "Your mom's right, Gavin. I love you, and I'm going to be around for a while. I-is that a good thing?"

Jenna didn't often see Cade unsure of himself. This small boy could make a tough Navy SEAL stutter with uncertainty.

Gavin nodded his head again, this time his smile stretching from ear to ear. "Are you gonna teach me swimming?"

"Yep. As soon as we get settled, we're going to find a pool and turn you into a fish."

Gavin giggled and squirmed off Cade's lap. He then proceeded to run around the room propelling his arms like a swimmer.

Jenna rolled her eyes. "I told you he needs work."

"He's been strapped in a car seat for too long. He needs some fresh air and exercise."

"Ball, ball, ball."

Jenna held a finger to her lips. "Shh. We might have neighbors."

She draped her arm around Cade's hunched shoulders and whispered in his ear. "You can relax now. That went great. No tantrums, no tears."

"Poor kid's probably just happy to have any father."

She pursed her lips. The man just wouldn't give himself a break. "But he doesn't have just any father. He has you, and he's very lucky."

Cade's phone buzzed in his front pocket and he snatched it, glancing at the display. "It's a cleared number, but I don't recognize it."

"Prospero?"

"Has to be."

He punched the talk button and listened, while Jenna's heart pounded in her chest.

He said, "Yeah."

The pause that followed went on forever, and Jenna tugged at his sleeve.

Cade held up his hand. "Yeah, I can be there, but give me some time. Eight o'clock will work. Tomorrow night. Everything in order?"

Jenna scrambled for the pad of paper and motel pen near the phone by the bed and held them out to Cade, but he shook his head and tapped his head with his forefinger.

"Got it." He ended the call, folding the phone between his hands.

"Well? Do they have a place for us?"

"Eventually."

Jenna licked her lips. "What does that mean?"

"It means we'll get our hideaway, once I show up at a meeting—a meeting where I could be the bait."

Chapter Thirteen

Jenna clutched his arm, knocking the phone from his grasp. "What does that mean?"

"That was an Agent Jeff Curson on the phone. They have new identities for us and a location, but we're supposed to meet him and Beth Warren to get our IDs, cash and new lives."

She released him and rubbed her palms on her thighs. "That's a good thing, right? You know Beth. You mentioned her before."

"Yeah."

"Why do you think you're going to be the bait?"

"I'm not sure." He scooped up his cell from the floor and tapped his chin with it. "Curson sounded…weird. If Prospero really does think I have the plans, this could be a setup."

"Is there someone else you can call? Your team members? Jack Coburn?"

"You heard J.D. He's out of the country. Gage is probably in South America and Deb's on leave right now. They're all scattered. Unavailable. I have to follow protocol. If Prospero is calling me in for a meeting, I have to be there. I have to assume this is coming from the very top."

"Gavin and I have to come, too?" She shot a glance at

Gavin, now sprawled on the bed next to them, rolling from edge to edge.

"I'm not leaving you here, not on your own. Not again."

"When and where?" She took a deep breath and straightened her spine.

"Arizona. Tomorrow." He massaged her neck. "We can stay here tonight and get an early start tomorrow morning."

She fell back on the bed. "We should've stayed in New Mexico. I feel like we're crisscrossing the Southwest."

"We could've used that helicopter."

"We could've used a lot of things."

A few hours later as the sun began to go down over the park, Cade had never felt so tired in a good way. They'd stopped at a drugstore and bought a cheap rubber ball, some bottles of water and some chewy fruit snacks that he'd never eaten before in his life. He liked them.

They'd played with that ball every which way. Played catch, kicked it like a soccer ball, shot a few hoops and even used a stick to bat it. The way his chest swelled with pride the first time Gavin caught the ball nearly knocked him off his feet.

How could he ever leave this boy again? Or this woman?

Jenna collapsed beside him after chasing Gavin up and down the slide. "I'm glad you were here to play with him. I'm exhausted already."

"Lightweight." He snapped his fingers. "I could do another two rounds."

She squeezed his biceps. "That's because you're a stud."

"Daddy, come push me." Gavin had scrambled onto a swing, his legs pumping the air above the sand.

Cade swallowed the ridiculous lump in his throat for about the fifth time that afternoon. Would he ever be able to hear that word from Gavin's lips without getting choked up?

"One more time, bud, and then we break for pizza."

As he struggled to his feet, Jenna mumbled, "Light-weight."

When they finished at the park, they stopped at a pizza place and took a couple of pizzas back to the motel. This might almost feel normal if they weren't all taking off to-morrow morning to get new identities.

Jenna plopped a slice of cheese pizza onto a paper plate for Gavin, sitting cross-legged in front of the TV, and shook her finger at him. "One cartoon while you eat, then bath and bedtime."

"Can we go to the park tomorrow?"

She sucked a strand of cheese from her finger. "We're driving again tomorrow, but we'll have lots of time to go to the park—after."

"And the swimming pool."

"And a swimming pool." Cade handed Gavin a bunch of napkins. "If you swim as good as you throw, you're going to be winning all kinds of races."

"Ah, don't get too competitive there, Dad," Jenna teased.

Cade stretched out on the floor next to Gavin and slid a piece of pepperoni pizza onto his own plate. "Maybe I'll be one of those fathers who screams and yells on the side-lines and gets kicked out of my kid's games."

"I'll keep you in line." She nudged his foot with her own.

Jenna was kidding, but Cade hung on to her words with a pathetic desperation. Could she really teach him to be a good father? He'd had the worst of role models—a man who would sell out his own flesh and blood for a couple of bucks.

They finished eating and Cade joined Jenna at the edge of the tub to wash the pizza stains from Gavin's face and scrub the dirt from beneath his fingernails. After one af-ternoon of hard play, Gavin seemed to accept him at his mother's side.

That was the thing about kids—good parenting, bad parenting, they didn't know the difference. Look at him. When he was a kid, he'd thought his father could do no wrong.

With Gavin toweled dry and snug in his pajamas, Jenna tucked him into the double bed on the other side of the nightstand from theirs. Then she cozied up to Cade, and all thoughts about how to be a good father flitted away. Now he wanted to be a good lover.

He slipped his arm around her shoulder and drew circles on the side of her breast with his thumb. She swiveled her hips toward him and threw one leg over his thigh. He slumped down, kissing the top of her head and edging his hand beneath the top of her pajamas. He flattened his hand against her belly, getting ready to make his next move.

Then the mattress dipped, and Gavin was wriggling his way between them.

Jenna smoothed her fingers across Gavin's cheek. "Don't you want to sleep in your own bed, honey bunny? Daddy and I will be right here in the bed next to yours."

He burrowed deeper between them. "Sleep here."

She lifted one brow at Cade. "Welcome to fatherhood."

Cade pulled the covers down, so Gavin could slip beneath them. "I can handle this."

Jenna sighed and rested her head on Cade's shoulder as the images from the TV flickered across her face. He kissed her again and adjusted his arm so that Gavin's head nestled in the crook of his elbow.

He could handle this.

The following morning, they left before sunrise. The crisp, cool air needled his skin as he loaded up the car with their meager belongings. How long would they have to hide out? It went against his nature, but he wanted to keep his wife and son safe. And this time, he wanted to stay with them.

He had to stay with them.

Jenna snapped on her seat belt and hitched her seat back in a reclining position. "Where are we meeting them?"

"At a warehouse."

"That sounds…weird."

"It's more private, out of the way. No cameras, no crowds."

"Is it going to be safe?"

"We're going to meet members of Prospero. We'll be safe."

"That's what we thought about that outpost in Arizona." Her gaze etched into his profile. "You're putting up a good front, but I can tell you're worried. Do you think they'll ambush you?"

He lifted his shoulders. "If they do, they'll just bring me in. Isn't that what we want, anyway?"

"That would mean they don't trust you."

"In our business, trust is in short supply. If they think I have the plans, all they can do is question me. I don't have them."

"What will they do with us? With me and Gavin?"

"They'll settle you like they're supposed to."

"But without you."

Over his dead body. "Once I'm cleared, I'll be joining you. Besides, we're jumping the gun here. Curson told me they have our new IDs, and I have to believe that."

"Until we find out otherwise."

"You've gotten suspicious over the years." He chucked her under the chin.

"It comes from being married to a spy."

"It's not a bad quality to have—even if you're married to an accountant."

She laced her fingers and stretched her arms in front of her. "Where do you think we'll get settled?"

"I have no idea. That's the point. Beth does a good job. She'll make sure it's someplace secure."

"I still won't be able to contact my family."

"Do you want to?" Jenna's family must've been the least of her worries when she went into hiding. She'd practically disowned them even before he'd met her.

She shrugged and hummed along to a song on the radio.

Maybe that's another reason why the two of them had bonded so quickly—they'd both given up on their families. He and Kyle still had ties, but distance and his career had made it difficult for them to keep in touch. Jenna and her sister still had a civil relationship, but her sister kept in close contact with their parents and Jenna didn't want any part of them.

How could her parents be any worse than Kevin?

Cade winced, the wound of his father's betrayal still fresh. His gaze wandered to the rearview mirror, where he caught a glimpse of Gavin, head tilted to the side in blissful sleep already. He'd had a terrible role model for parenting in Kevin, but Jenna could be his new role model. She'd done a great job with their son so far.

A golden hue washed across the horizon, and Cade reached for his sunglasses. He had to be a better father than Kevin. He couldn't possibly be much worse.

They had to make their way back through New Mexico and Albuquerque, heading down the 25, and Cade couldn't help it if his foot got heavier on the accelerator as they sped through the cold, dry landscape.

He'd never forget the look in Kevin's eyes when he'd proposed they trick Zendaris out of some money, putting Gavin at risk. The man had been dead inside even before Zendaris's men took his life.

They could make a few stops along the way to their final destination in Arizona. Cade had suggested meeting at eight o'clock to make sure he and Jenna had enough time to get there. He'd still held off on telling Curson their current location. He couldn't shake the feeling that something was off.

Cade had no intention of staying at a hotel close to the warehouse where the meeting was taking place. He needed distance and independence.

In case something went wrong.

After fiddling with the radio to find a station, Jenna tapped his wrist. "I can do some driving. You've been at it for hours."

"I'm not tired."

"Maybe not, but you could stretch out your legs on this side."

"We can stop for lunch." He checked the clock on the dashboard. "We have time."

"You never mentioned which part of Arizona."

"Didn't I?" He yawned. He knew Jenna hated it when he kept her in the dark, but he always figured the less she knew at any given time, the safer she'd be. "Down south, south of Tucson."

"Was it their idea to meet at night?"

"I wanted to make sure we could get there by the end of the day." He tucked a stray strand of hair behind her ear. "Don't worry. This is what we were waiting for, remember?"

"I just wonder why it took Prospero so long to get back to you after Jim murdered his coworker."

"Maybe we'll find out tonight. Maybe it doesn't matter." He pointed to a sign for gas and food. "Do you want to stop for lunch?"

"Only if you let me drive after we eat. This is not the most comfortable car in the world, especially for a guy your size."

"But it sure looked good sitting by the side of the road, didn't it?"

"Like a limousine."

"You should know. You traveled in a lot of those."

Jenna stuck out her tongue. "Don't remind me. My parents were so ostentatious, but then so were all their friends, so it didn't matter."

"Have they wondered where you've been? Do they know about Gavin?" He turned down the radio. Jenna had always hated discussing her family.

"I haven't contacted them at all." She crossed an ankle over her bouncing knee. "They're not my favorite people, but that doesn't mean I want arms dealers and terrorists paying them visits. It just seemed for the best that they not know about Gavin or about my life."

"Have they made any attempts to track you down?"

She lifted a brow in his direction. "Who hasn't?"

"Seriously."

"Seriously, I don't know. Maybe—" she waved her hands around the car "—someday I'll introduce them to Gavin. They're the only grandparents he has...now."

Cade's jaw tightened. "I wouldn't honor Kevin with that title."

She drew invisible patterns on the window. "I've been thinking, Cade. What if Zendaris's men killed Kevin because he wouldn't give you up?"

His stomach flip-flopped. Had that thought been in the back of his mind, too? He didn't want it there. He didn't want any more hope associated with Kevin. He'd burned out all the hope he had.

"That's giving the old man the benefit of the doubt. He'd already told me he was willing to play let's make a deal with Zendaris."

"He could've had a change of heart."

Cade snorted. "That would mean he had to have a heart. I thought we were talking about *your* family."

"From one dysfunctional set to another." She sighed and rubbed her figures from the glass.

"At least your parents aren't criminals."

"Oh, I don't know. They sure love money. In their own way, they love it as much as Kevin did."

"Not enough to sacrifice their only grandchild." Cade's palms felt slick on the steering wheel, and he turned the heat down in the car.

"I still think Zendaris's men killed Kevin because he wouldn't deliver."

"Or couldn't deliver." He took the next off-ramp, and the little car shuddered as he reduced his speed around the curve.

He pulled into the parking lot of a halfway decent diner that sported a few Peterbilts on the fringes. "You know what they say about dining with truckers."

"Let's just hope it's true. I'm starving." She twisted in her seat to jiggle Gavin's leg. "Wake up. Time for lunch."

It took her a few more tries before Gavin peeled one eye open. "Park."

"Not yet, but we'll go to another park soon." She smiled at Cade. "He must've been dreaming about our day at the park."

He wasn't the only one. Cade would never forget that day, even though he planned to have many more. "We'll have a lot of days at the park, Gavin."

"Swimming pool." Gavin rubbed his eyes and yawned.

"Yeah, that, too."

"Don't start asking your daddy for too much." She winked at Cade. "I don't think he could refuse you anything right now."

And why should he? He'd already refused him so much.

They ate and got back on the road, this time with Jenna behind the wheel.

Cade shoved the seat back and stretched his legs as far as he could in the small car. He closed his eyes but knew sleep would evade him. He hadn't had a good night's sleep since...hell, he didn't even know.

Yeah, he did. Since two nights ago, after he and Jenna had made love. Then he'd slept like the dead—while his father was dying.

As the pale, wintry sun said its farewell to the day and dark blue night suffused the sky, they sped through Tucson. They were able to shed their parkas and gloves again. Jenna was right. They'd been speeding back and forth across the Southwest so many times that Cade felt like a yo-yo.

He'd taken over the driving duties again, and Jenna was on the lookout for a hotel.

She squinted out the window. "So, we want to be close to the meeting place, but not too close."

"That's right. Anyplace around here should do it. Extra points for finding a place with a pool."

Jenna put her finger to her lips and glanced over her shoulder at Gavin pressing his nose against the window, oblivious to their conversation. "Don't get him started."

They found a hotel with an indoor pool. Because they had a few hours before their meeting, Cade took Gavin into the pool while Jenna watched from the deck.

"I'd join you, but I don't have any shorts, and I think I'd get arrested if wore my underwear in the pool like Gavin."

Cade wiggled his eyebrows up and down. "I wouldn't arrest you."

Gavin squealed and splashed as Cade held on to his arms and pulled him around the pool. "See? He's a natural."

"Looks like a natural splasher to me."

"Your mom doesn't understand the finer points of swimming." He launched Gavin into the air, and he splashed Jenna when he landed.

"Flying." Gavin's screech echoed in the enclosed area.

"You like flying?" Cade tossed him up a few more times until Jenna interrupted.

"We'd better get going. Don't want to keep—" she looked both ways at two bunches of families in the pool and cupped her hand around her mouth "—Prospero waiting."

Cade pulled Gavin onto his shoulders and swam to the edge of the pool. Whatever happened tonight, wherever Prospero sent them, he'd turn this life with his family into a reality.

Back in the room after a quick shower, Cade yanked a black beanie over his ears, and Jenna crept up behind him and ran her finger between the cap and his head. "You look…stealthy."

"Habit. I want to blend into the night."

She hugged herself and hunched her shoulders. "Will we come in with you or wait in the car?"

"Wait in the car at first, but you'll have to come inside the warehouse. They'll need pictures for the new IDs."

She caught his eye in the mirror. "What happens if it's some sort of trap for you?"

"Even if Prospero does suspect me of having the plans and this is a trap, they'll still do right by you and Gavin and get you settled."

"Without you."

"I can convince them I don't have the plans if that's what they believe. Once I do that, they'll release me and I'll join you and Gavin." He turned and kissed the lines forming between her brows. "Don't worry. This is going to be a piece of cake."

Jenna pulled a sweatshirt over Gavin's head, and they

packed their bags and loaded them in the car in case Prospero wanted them to leave Arizona immediately.

Cade's neck tightened as he drove across town to an industrial area. He'd rather be meeting in a hotel room, but at least he could enter this abandoned warehouse with his weapon drawn. No chance of doing that in a hotel.

Not that he believed he'd need his weapon. Not against Prospero.

He pulled around a corner housing several warehouses plunked in the middle of a semi-lit parking lot, deserted except for a rusty car in the front and a truck along the side. Must be Curson's truck.

"This is it?" Jenna's voice quavered and she cleared her throat. "This is it?"

"This is the place." He pulled into a parking space several feet away from the truck. A sliver of light razored across the asphalt where a door to the warehouse had been propped open.

That was a good sign, wasn't it?

"They must be in there. Looks like some kind of office attached to the warehouse."

A noisy sigh escaped Jenna's lips. "Okay, you first."

"Do me a favor." He cut the engine and reached for his weapon beneath his seat. "Get Gavin out of his car seat and duck down with him."

"To dodge the bullets?"

"Just to be on the safe side." He flicked the keys still hanging in the ignition. "I'm leaving these here, too."

"Just to be on the safe side."

"That's right." He pinched her chin, opened the car door and then leaned back in to kiss her. *Just to be on the safe side.*

He locked the car doors before he planted his feet on

the ground, and then shut the door behind him as quietly as he could.

Holding his weapon in front of him with both hands, he crept toward the propped-open door. His nostrils flared. Was that gunpowder?

His grip tightened on his gun and he threw a glance over his shoulder at the dimly lit parking lot. No other cars squealing into the lot, no stealthy figures creeping around—except him.

He tapped the barrel of his gun against the door, leaned his shoulder against it and eased it open. The smell of gunpowder permeated the air even more in this enclosed space, and his heart thudded against his rib cage.

Long-forgotten papers and registers littered the gray, metal shelves lining the office. A single green-shaded lamp burned on the battered desk and more papers, neatly stacked this time, were lined up in a row on the desktop.

Pushing the door wider, he stepped into the room. The door creaked, announcing his presence, so he called out. "Hello?"

A moan answered him.

His mouth dry and his pulse racing, Cade stepped around the desk and froze.

The body of a man lay sprawled across the cement floor, blood meandering away from his head.

Now he knew why it smelled like gunpowder.

Chapter Fourteen

The man was dead. Cade could tell that from here. The moan hadn't come from him.

Cade shifted his gaze to the figure of a woman crumpled against the wall, her head tilted to the side. One leg, stretched in front of her, jerked and she moaned again.

Cade backed up against the wall, his gun tracking from side to side in the small office. A window in the office faced the darkened warehouse. The grubby door next to the window sported a dead bolt. Nobody would be coming in from the warehouse.

He turned back to the entryway to get a clear view of the parking lot and his car. It looked empty. Jenna was doing a good job of keeping herself and Gavin hidden from view, but he didn't want her out there on her own.

Not with a killer in the vicinity.

He glanced at the woman—must be Beth. He'd help her once he secured Jenna and Gavin.

He jogged back to the car, his gaze constantly darting around the parking lot. He tapped on the window, and Jenna's head popped up. He pointed to the lock and she reached over and unlocked the car.

He stuck his head inside. "We've got a problem. I need your help."

Her eyes took over her face. "What's wrong?"

"Bring Gavin and come inside."

She clambered out of the car first and scooped up a drowsy Gavin.

He didn't want Gavin to see Jeff Curson dead on the floor of the office. How many dead bodies could a kid see in one week before he started putting two and two together?

Gripping Jenna by the arm, he led her into the office and pointed to the swivel chair behind the desk. "Park Gavin in that chair."

Gavin curled his legs beneath him, folding an arm beneath his head—not sleeping, but close enough.

Jenna's face paled before she even peered around the desk. "What's that smell?"

"The gunpowder?"

She shook her head, wrinkling her nose. "It's…it's…" She covered her mouth with her hand as she stepped past him into the office. "Blood."

Cade pulled the office door shut with a click and locked it behind him. Now they couldn't be ambushed in here.

Jenna seemed fixated on Jeff's corpse, so Cade nudged her side. "Beth's in the corner and she's still alive."

Jenna jerked her head to the right. "Oh, my God. Why haven't you helped her?"

She rushed to Beth and crouched down beside her.

"I didn't want to leave you and Gavin in the car after I discovered this scene. I wanted to secure us inside first. How is she?"

Jenna's fingers tapped around Beth's head. "Looks like a head injury from behind—a blow to the head."

"She was moaning before." Cade finally kneeled on the cold floor next to Jeff and felt for his nonexistent pulse.

"Beth? Beth? Can you hear me?"

Beth gasped and sobbed.

"It's okay. You're okay." Jenna twisted her head over her

shoulder. "Do you have any bandages in the car? Can you get a bottle of water?"

Cade patted Jeff's pockets. Jeff's holster was still strapped to his body, his weapon secured. He hadn't been expecting whatever calamity befell him tonight.

Cade jerked his thumb over his shoulder at the half-empty, five-gallon water bottle on its stand. "Use that."

"It's not very sterile."

"I think it's more important now to staunch any bleeding." He shrugged out of his windbreaker, yanked off his shirt and tugged his T-shirt over his head. He ripped it in two and tossed the pieces toward Jenna. "She's conscious?"

"Barely." Jenna folded one piece of his T-shirt into a square and held it against the back of Beth's head. "We need to get her out of here and clean her wound."

Cade pulled a few papers out of Jeff's pockets. *What had happened here?* A small camera lay in pieces just under the desk. The papers and forms on top of the desk had come from Prospero, but there was no sign of any travel documents, IDs or passports.

A bead of sweat ran down his spine.

Beth groaned, her legs shifting on the cement floor.

"Shh, it's okay." Jenna thumbed open Beth's eyelids and placed two fingers on her wrist. "Her pulse is strong."

Cade swept up all the papers on the desk and pocketed the broken camera. He also lifted Jeff's cell phone from his pocket and deposited it in his own. Next, he took his weapon.

He cracked open the door and poked his head into the parking lot. "We need to get out of here before their assailants return. Take these papers and Gavin back to the car and leave the back door open. I'll carry Beth out."

Jenna shook out the other piece of his T-shirt and wrapped it around Beth's head, tucking in the corner. "She needs some water or something stronger and about a half bottle of ibuprofen."

"We'll take care of her." He waved the papers at her. "Take these."

Once Jenna had Gavin clutched against her chest and the papers clamped against her body with one arm, Cade watched while she returned to the car.

Still gripping his gun, Cade slid his arms beneath Beth's limp form and hoisted her up. He said a silent prayer as he stepped over Jeff's body and out of the office.

He made a beeline for the gaping car door, one refrain thrumming through his head—*get Jenna and Gavin out of here.*

Gavin was sleeping in his car seat. He probably wouldn't remember one minute of this nightmare visit to the warehouse. Cade placed Beth on the seat next to Gavin and pulled the seat belt across her body, clicking it into place.

He tucked a blanket around Beth's inert form even though her skin was warm to the touch. She'd stopped moaning and moving and her even breathing gave him hope. Blood from the nasty cut on her head had soaked through the T-shirt bandage, but otherwise she looked as if she could be taking a nap like Gavin.

"How's she doing?"

"She drifted into unconsciousness, but her vital signs are good. She could be sleeping." He tossed the car keys to Jenna and rounded the car to the passenger side. "You drive while I keep watch."

"I-if someone was here, he'd have made himself known by now." She slid into the driver's seat, cranked on the engine and lurched out of the parking lot. Despite her statement, she must've felt the urgency, too.

"Who knows? If we had more time and the light of day, I wouldn't have minded taking a look around the warehouse.

Are there other tire tracks? Bullet casings? A weapon used against Beth? We can't exactly treat this as a crime scene."

"And you'll just leave Jeff there?"

"Prospero will do…cleanup."

She shook her head. "That sounds so clinical. Jeff probably had a wife and a family, a life."

Jenna slowed the car as she neared the freeway on-ramps. "Where to?"

Cade checked the side mirror. They'd been going solo since leaving the warehouse. Whoever attacked Jeff and Beth hadn't waited around for an encore. Why? If Zendaris had gotten a line on this meeting tonight, he had to know Cade would be there with Jenna and Gavin to pick up the IDs, which had been confiscated.

"Let's go back to our hotel. Beth needs some attention."

"Should we take her to a hospital? The emergency room docs don't have to know what happened. We can tell them she slipped and fell."

"And if she comes to while there? If she starts babbling? We don't involve local law enforcement. Ever. They may even make a connection between her and that body in the warehouse."

"You mean Jeff." Her lips tightened.

"Yeah, Jeff." He massaged his temples. "Don't think we don't mourn our own, Jenna. Don't think we ever forget."

"You inhabit a different world from the rest of us." She accelerated on the highway toward lights and activity. "We can stop at a drugstore and pick up some first-aid supplies. But if she doesn't fully regain consciousness, we'll have to take her somewhere."

"Agreed. Pull off when you see that shopping center we passed on the way to the warehouse."

Jenna glanced at Cade's profile, which seemed carved from stone. He could be so caring and engaged with her and Gavin and then turn into…this. It worried her, but she supposed this cool, calm detachment trumped wailing and gnashing of teeth.

His cool and calm had kept them alive so far.

She squeezed the steering wheel and blew out a breath. "Do you know her well—Beth?"

"She joined Prospero about the same time I did. She's good with numbers. She's a good analyst. She's the one who found a place for us based on statistics and probabilities. I guess she didn't adequately calculate the risk of meeting us in a deserted warehouse."

"Does she have family?"

Cade gave her a sharp look. "Why this sudden interest in everyone's families?"

"I just can't help thinking if you were on an assignment and got injured or—worse—would someone know to contact me? Would some agent just abandon your body?"

He clasped his hand around hers. "Prospero knows all next of kin. All agents and support people know the risks, and we're willing to take them."

"But you don't own the risk, not alone." She pounded her chest with one fist. "We share the risk—your spouses, your children, your siblings and parents."

"Do you want me to say I take it all back? Do you want me to say I wish I'd never met you, married you, had this incredible boy with you?" He stroked her cheek with the back of his hand. "I won't do it. Call me selfish, but I won't do it."

Jenna let out a little sob, and then she sealed her lips. That ended the self-pity. That ended the blame. She loved Cade fiercely. If she had to share him with this life of his and all the danger and uncertainty that came with it, she'd do it. But Gavin…Gavin deserved more.

"That big shopping center is coming up. Take this exit."

Jenna pulled off the highway and curved around to a parallel street. She read off each lighted sign until she found one for a drugstore.

When she parked, Cade dropped his heavy weapon in her lap. "You know how to release the safety, right?"

She nodded. "I take it I'm staying here."

"Keep an eye out. I'll run inside and get some first-aid supplies for Beth. Anyone approaches the car, shoot first and ask questions later."

Tracing the butt of the gun, she said, "Nothing like drawing attention to yourself."

Cade exited the car and waited while she locked it. She eyed the pedestrians crisscrossing the parking lot from store to store, shopping for books and groceries, and heading to the movies in the corner of the lot. She hoped none of them decided to ask her for directions.

Beth exhaled and coughed.

Jenna jumped and twisted in her seat. "Beth? Beth? Come out of it, Beth."

The woman groaned and raised a hand to her head, brushing dark brown hair matted with blood from her face. "No. Jeff."

"Beth, it's okay now. You're safe." Jenna unsnapped her seat belt and placed one knee on the console as she extended a bottle of water to the wounded woman in the backseat. "Can you drink?"

Beth's eyes fluttered open. She widened them in terror and put up her hands.

Catching Beth's fluttering hands with her own, Jenna soothed. "It's going to be fine. Cade's with us. You know Cade Stark, right?"

Beth went limp and smacked her lips as if trying to get them to work properly.

Jenna pressed the bottle of water into the other woman's hand. "Drink this."

Beth put the bottle to her mouth and drank deeply. She coughed and a trickle of water dripped off her chin. Her eyes filled with tears and one rolled down her cheek to join the water.

Jenna scrambled for her purse on the floor of the car. "Are you in pain? I have some ibuprofen."

Beth whispered. "A-are you Cade's wife?"

Relief made Jenna feel lightheaded. "Yes. I'm Jenna. Do you remember now? You and…Jeff were meeting us to give us new IDs."

"I remember—that part."

Uh-oh. If she didn't remember the rest of what happened in that warehouse, Cade would be sorely disappointed. She finally popped the lid off the small bottle of ibuprofen and shook one into her hand, glanced at Beth and shook another one into her hand. "Take these. That's a vicious gash on your head. Must hurt like heck."

Beth swallowed the gel caps with a gulp of water. "Thanks… Cade?"

"He's inside picking up some supplies." Jenna sucked in her lower lip. "He didn't think it was a good idea to bring you to the emergency room, but we would have if things had gone south for you."

"No hospitals. No police. We know the drill. Even the Prospero techs and support people know the drill."

With each passing minute, Beth's voice got stronger and her gaze more focused. She turned toward Gavin and put her hand on the car seat. "Cade's son."

"Yes, that's Gavin. Thank God he slept through the chaos at the warehouse."

Beth wrinkled her brow and ran her fingertips along the edge of the makeshift bandage. "Chaos. Jeff?"

"I'm sorry. Jeff's dead."

Beth pressed her hand against her mouth, smothering a cry. "Gunfire. They shot him."

"Who, Beth? What did they want?"

The tap on the window made both women jump. Cade's hand rested against the glass, a plastic bag dangling from his wrist.

Jenna unlocked the door for him and stated the obvious. "Beth regained consciousness."

He wedged the bag onto the console. "Thank God. Is it just your head? Are you injured anywhere else?"

"I—I don't think so. It's good to see you alive and well, Cade. We've…some of us have been worried about you."

"And we've been worried about you." He reached into the bag. "Jeff didn't make it."

"I know. Your—Jenna told me."

He plucked a bottle out of the bag and shook it. "Ibuprofen?"

"I already got some. How's the injury on my head?"

"Not sure. Jenna wrapped it to stop the bleeding. Lots of blood, but then that's heads for you. Your vitals never wavered, so I took that as a good sign. Or we would've taken you to the emergency room."

She held up a hand. "You don't have to explain anything to me, Agent Stark. I know how it works."

Jenna started the car. "I'm going to get Beth back to our hotel room so we can take a look at that injury."

As she pulled out of the parking lot, Cade took a deep breath and started in with the questioning. He couldn't wait until they cleaned the blood out of her hair?

"What happened back there, Beth? Who ambushed you two and why? If it was Zendaris's men, why didn't they stick around for us?" He circled his finger in the air to encompass himself, her and Gavin. "And what happened to our documents?"

Beth closed her eyes and pressed two fingers against her forehead. "Can you give me a minute or two? I'm feeling dizzy all of a sudden."

"Must've been all those questions." Jenna gave Cade the evil eye and drew a finger across her throat. "We're not far from the hotel. Let Beth rest, and let's properly dress her wound. Then you can ask all the questions you want."

"We need to know if Jeff's killers are still in the area, what they plan to do."

"They didn't follow us from the warehouse, and there's no way they know where we're staying. Let's give it a rest for tonight."

Cade glanced from her to Beth, her eyes still closed, and shrugged. "I guess it can wait."

Twenty minutes later, Jenna drove the car into the parking structure, the tires squealing on the cement floor of the garage. She found a spot near the elevator.

"Can you walk, Beth?"

"I'm sure I can." She touched Gavin's nose. "Your little guy has been out like a light the entire time. Must be nice to sleep like that—the sleep of innocence."

Jenna took the plastic bags from Cade while he gathered Gavin into his arms. Jenna slung her purse over her shoulder, hooking the bags around her arms. She then dipped into the backseat to help Beth out of the car.

Beth winced as she struggled to stand.

Jenna took her arm to steady her. "Are you sure you can do this? Cade could carry you inside."

Beth snorted. "Hardly keeping a low profile. I can manage. Just hang on to my arm like we're old friends."

"Any friend of Cade's is a friend of mine, so we *are* old friends." She pulled Beth's arm through the crook of her own, offering a shoulder for Beth to lean on. "We'll take it slowly."

Beth's trauma hadn't affected her balance, and while she kept a tight hold of Jenna's arm, she managed to walk beside her back up to the room.

Jenna settled Beth at the small table by the window. "Unless you want to lie down on the bed."

"This is fine. I don't want to get blood on those nice white pillows." Beth turned her head from side to side. "Looks like you'd already checked out of this place."

Cade tucked Gavin under the covers of one of the double beds. "We took our stuff in case we had to leave from the warehouse. Is it okay if Gavin falls asleep without brushing his teeth again?"

"I brushed them before we left." She dug into the plastic bag from the drugstore and put a bottle of alcohol, a roll of bandages and a pair of scissors on the table. "I'm going to get a washcloth from the bathroom."

"I'll go down to the car and bring our bags back up."

After Cade left the room, Jenna engaged the chain. Then she grabbed two washcloths from the stack on the glass shelf above the sink. She soaked one with warm water and returned to Beth, sitting at the table gazing at Gavin.

"Must be hard on him, huh?"

Jenna shrugged. She was done piling the guilt on Cade. She wasn't going to lay into him again with one of his co-workers. "It's true what the experts say. Kids are amazingly resilient. Gavin's life is in turmoil right now, but he has two loving parents, and he just discovered he had a daddy. Now, sit still."

With tentative fingers, Jenna brushed Beth's dark hair to the side. Clotted blood flowered out from a deep gash. "Ouch. What did they hit you with?"

"I have no idea. All I know is it hurt like hell."

Jenna dabbed the wet washcloth around the wound to clean off the blood. "You might need stitches."

When she'd cleaned the cut, Jenna drenched the second washcloth with alcohol. "Sorry, this is going to sting."

"All for the greater good." Beth squeezed her eyes shut and clenched her jaw.

By the time Cade returned to the room with the bags, Jenna had cleaned and bandaged Beth's head. "She has a bad cut and some swelling, but she seems fine."

Beth waved her away. "I'm okay. Thanks for your help."

Cade dropped the bags in the corner of the room, dipped into the minibar and emerged with a couple of bottles of booze in one hand and some mixers in the other. "Straight or with a splash of juice or soda water?"

"Is there bourbon among one of those lovely little bottles?"

He pinched one bottle by the neck and held it up. "Only the finest."

"I'll take one of those—straight."

Cade reached for a glass, but Beth stopped him. "I mean straight from the bottle. Hand it over."

He set the bottle on the table in front of her with a click. "What happened in there?"

Beth unscrewed the lid and tipped half the contents down her throat. She wrinkled her nose and cleared her throat. "God, I needed that."

"Start from the beginning. Where were you going to settle us?"

"A midsize town up in Oregon—big enough to get lost in, small enough to keep track of your neighbors and co-workers. I've found that's the ideal situation."

Jenna pulled out the chair across from Beth and sat down. She could be an analyst for Prospero because that's exactly the program she'd followed when hopping from place to place. "You had everything ready for us?"

"We had ID—social security cards, birth certificates and

we were ready to prepare drivers' licenses once we took your pictures. We even had a variety of disguises for you in case you wanted to use them going forward."

"All that was gone when we got there." Cade ran a hand through his hair and clenched the back of his neck.

"They took it."

"Who's *they,* Beth?"

"Jeff and I were setting everything up, waiting for you. Jeff didn't have his weapon drawn because he was just expecting you."

Cade crossed his arms and wedged a shoulder against the window. "You should always expect the worst."

Beth took a small sip of the bourbon and continued. "We'd left the door to the office open for you. I had my back to the door and the next thing I knew, a couple of people in black ski masks burst in. They shot Jeff. I turned toward the warehouse and that's when they clobbered me."

"What do you think they hit you with?" Cade drew his brows together. "I didn't see any weapon on the floor."

"All I know is that it was hard." She ran her fingers along her bandage. "I didn't even see them come at me."

Jenna squeezed Beth's hand. "You were lucky they didn't shoot you, too."

"That's what's puzzling me." Cade scratched the stubble on his chin. "Why didn't they just shoot you, too, and be done with it? And why didn't they wait for us? We would've been walking right into a trap."

Beth spread her hands. "I can't tell you any of that. Maybe they wanted me alive to tell the story. Maybe they just took out Jeff because he had the gun. Maybe they just wanted to disrupt the relocation plan."

"Zendaris wants more than that. He wants those plans back and he wants Gavin in order to force my hand. If his men had any idea I was going to be at that warehouse with Jenna and Gavin, they would've lain in wait for us."

"Oh, no." Beth's eyes grew round, and she covered her mouth. "Don't you see, Cade?"

Jenna's pulse beat double time, and she ran her tongue around her mouth.

"That wasn't a Zendaris ambush. It couldn't be, for all those reasons you mentioned."

Cade shurgged off the window and stalked to the table. "What do you mean?"

"Zendaris's people had no way of knowing we were meeting you and Jenna at that warehouse, and you're right, they would've never left without your son."

"Spit it out, Beth."

"That was an inside job, Cade. Someone at Prospero doesn't want to see you resettled. Someone at Prospero doesn't want to see you or your family safe."

Chapter Fifteen

Hot rage thumped through Cade's veins, and a red haze clouded his vision.

There it was in plain view for all to see. Prospero didn't trust him. Jack Coburn didn't trust him. Had J.D. been lying to him, too?

"Wait." Jenna held up her hands. "That doesn't make sense, either. If Prospero believes Cade still has those anti-drone plans, they would've stayed in that warehouse and captured him. Why kill Jeff at that point?"

How quickly she'd leaped to his defense. Her words dampened his anger, and he took a deep, shuddering breath.

Beth put a hand to her head. "Jeff and I weren't in on any other plan except to deliver the IDs and your new location to you."

"But if the powers that be at Prospero told you what they had planned for me, you still would've gone ahead with the meeting, right? It's not for you to question authority, and they know that. They'd have no reason *not* to tell you."

Cade crossed his arms and bunched his fists against his biceps to keep from hitting the wall.

"I don't know, Cade. The powers that be, as you call them, have been acting strangely lately. They're wondering, along with everyone else, why the people who stole the plans from you haven't come forward yet to offer them on the world market."

Jenna hopped up from the table and paced the room. "Maybe the people who stole the plans aren't interested in selling them. Maybe they're interested in developing the weapon. They could've been Zendaris's customers, and instead of paying a fortune to an arms dealer, they decided to steal them."

Cade tugged on his ear. "That makes sense. I just wish they'd step forward so Zendaris would get off your tail."

Jenna stopped pacing and twisted her hands in front of her. "Why would they step forward? The heat's off them. They're free to develop the anti-drone in secret without interference."

"That does make sense, Jenna." Beth traced the rim of the bourbon bottle with her fingertip. "But what just happened in the warehouse?"

"I don't know." Cade raked a hand through his hair, feeling as if he'd taken a blow to the head himself. He didn't know what to think and he couldn't shake the feeling that he didn't have all the facts from Prospero. A big piece of this whole puzzle was missing.

Beth finished off the booze and spun the empty bottle on the table. "Did you send a message to Prospero about what went down in the warehouse?"

"Yes."

"Did you get confirmation?"

"Yes."

"Nothing else? No new meeting scheduled?" Beth's gaze never left the spinning bottle.

"No."

She smacked her hand against the bottle to stop it. "That town in Oregon was my first choice, but it wasn't the only choice."

Cade took Jenna's arm and pulled her toward the bed. Her fidgeting scattered his thoughts even more. "What are you proposing, Beth?"

"I'm proposing—" she hunched forward in her seat "—that we finish the job. That I get you and your family settled."

"The IDs?"

She grinned and patted her bag, the one she'd been clutching on the floor of the warehouse office. "Jed Moran wasn't the only ID I had picked out for you. I made a couple of extras with different names in case you had any objection to the one I picked for you."

"Are you telling me you have some extra IDs in your purse?"

"I do." She plunged a hand into her bag. "I don't have the camera anymore or the laminator, so I can't get a picture ID for you, but I have a couple of social security cards and a birth certificate for Gavin."

Cade bounded off the bed and kissed her forehead on the other side of her bandage. "You're brilliant."

Beth's pale skin reddened under his attentions. "Just thorough. I propose we go on to plan B, and I'll return to Prospero once we've implemented it."

"Are you going to tell Prospero where we are?" Jenna clasped her hands between her knees.

"I wasn't supposed to tell them, anyway." Beth shrugged. "Only Jeff and I knew your new identities and location. And Jeff's gone." She sniffled and rubbed her nose.

Cade clasped her hand. "God, I'm sorry, Beth. You and Jeff were more than coworkers?"

Her blush deepened and her lashes fluttered. "Just friends, but good friends."

"We appreciate your help, Beth." Jenna rose from the bed and hovered behind her. "Where is the location of plan B?"

"Closer than Oregon. In fact, we can take that little car you have out to Texas."

Jenna groaned. "More driving?"

"But this time, you're going home. You can enroll Gavin in school, get jobs, settle down."

Jenna scrunched up her face. "Gavin's only three. He has two years before he starts school, and I hope we'll be in our real home before then."

"Of course." Beth's gaze wandered to Cade's as if they shared knowledge Jenna couldn't possibly comprehend... and maybe they did.

It could be years before the people in possession of the plans developed a weapon to use against the drones, years during which Zendaris would still believe Cade had those plans or at least that he'd sold them to someone else.

Men without honor had no difficulty believing other men shared their lack of conscience. Look at Kevin. He actually thought Cade would go along with his dangerous scheme.

He rapped his knuckles on the table. "Then Texas here we come. I even have a pair of cowboy boots."

Beth laughed, which was a good sign, even though it was accompanied by a little wince.

"J.D. would be so proud of you. Remember that one Christmas party where he showed up wearing a black cowboy hat, black boots with silver-tipped toes and a huge silver buckle on his belt? Then he spent the entire party saying things like *y'all* and *darn tootin'* just to bother you? We all thought you were going to strangle him."

"I do remember that. We had some good times at those parties."

Jenna huffed out a breath. "I wouldn't know. I never got a chance to go to one."

Cade rose from the table and hung an arm around Jenna's shoulder. "You could've gone to the Christmas party, but it was in D.C. and I distinctly remember you were working that weekend—flying to London or something."

"Don't think I would've had the stomach for J.D., anyway."

"How about Texas? Do you think you have the stomach for Texas?"

She threaded her fingers through his and pulled his hand to her lips. "As long as I have you and Gavin with me, anyplace is paradise. How far?"

"West of Dallas, so it's less than a fifteen-hour drive. We should turn in now if we want to get an early start." Beth pushed back from her chair and gripped the edge of the table, swaying.

Cade pulled away from Jenna and steadied Beth. "Are you okay? Still dizzy?"

"Just a little. I'll go down to the front desk and get my own room."

"No way." Cade pointed to the bed not occupied by Gavin. "You can have that bed tonight, and Jenna and I will share with Gavin. Won't be the first time, and my guess is it won't be the last."

Beth's gaze darted to Jenna's face. "I don't want to intrude."

"Don't be ridiculous. You suffered a serious injury tonight and the loss of your friend. We're not going to allow you to be on your own."

"We don't have much, but we even have an extra toothbrush." He pulled a bag from the drugstore out of the suitcase and handed it to Beth. "Help yourself."

"Thanks, Cade...and Jenna. I'm going to get you two settled if it's the last thing I do for Prospero."

Cade smiled his thanks, but it masked more uneasiness. Why would settling him and Jenna be the last thing Beth did for Prospero? She didn't really believe that by giving him and Jenna a new life she was going against the wishes of Prospero.

Did she?

JENNA LAY AWAKE AND STARED at the blinking red light on the smoke detector. With each double blink, she repeated *Tex-as, Tex-as, Tex-as.*

Would the Lone Star State be their refuge? They needed a refuge. They needed to slow down, live their lives, stop running. But she couldn't imagine Cade ever being satisfied with that kind of life.

Beth had mentioned getting jobs in their new location. Jenna missed her job as a flight attendant, but she'd take any job to support Gavin and keep him safe. Would Cade?

Had he worked so hard all those years to get into the Naval Academy, to get through Navy SEAL training, to become a member of Prospero only to throw it all away for some other job that could never satisfy him? Would he come to resent her and Gavin for tying him to an ordinary life?

Maybe they should go on like before. She and Gavin could live in hiding, and Cade could go back to his life as a Prospero agent.

If they'd take him.

What was the meaning of the silence on their end? Cade had explained to her that his contact with Prospero did not include lengthy conversations on the phone. Rather, that cell phone functioned as a vehicle for coded communications.

Coded or not, Cade hadn't been receiving much in the way of communications from Prospero. And now Beth seemed to be cut off, as well.

Jenna sighed and tugged Gavin's body across hers and onto the other side of her, so she could snuggle up against Cade. She wrapped one arm and one leg around his strong frame and kissed his sleeping face.

Beth echoed her sigh from the other bed and Jenna froze. Was someone else having trouble sleeping this night? She whispered. "Beth?"

Silence.

Nope, it would appear that she was the only restless sleeper in this room. She rolled to her other side and spooned against Cade while tugging Gavin's back against her. There. Between her two favorite guys in the world, she had to fall asleep.

The following morning, Jenna woke up to someone tapping her nose. She opened one eye and met a pair of brown eyes, fringed with stubby dark lashes.

"Mommy, there's a lady in our room."

She pinched Gavin's nose. "I know that. She's a friend and she needed a place to stay last night. She's going to come with us today to a new place."

"Is she bleeding?"

Jenna's stomach lurched. Gavin hadn't forgotten Sonia's body at the Arizona outpost. "No, she's fine."

That wasn't quite true. Beth probably still had a bloody bandage stuck to her head.

The mattress dipped behind her, and Cade scratched her cheek with his beard. "What are you two planning?"

Gavin scrambled over Jenna and wormed his way between her and Cade into his rightful place. He cupped his little hand over Cade's ear and said, "There's a lady over there."

"That's Beth. Do you remember when we, uh, picked her up last night?"

"I was sleeping in the car."

"That's right, you were. She hit her head last night, so we picked her up and brought her here."

Gavin wrinkled his nose. "She's bleeding?"

"A little. She's okay." Cade raised his brows at Jenna over Gavin's head.

"Like the lady in the bed. Like Marti." Gavin turned so suddenly that he bumped Jenna's chin with the top of his head. "Where's Marti?"

"She's back in Lovett Peak." Jenna held up her hand to play patty-cake, and Gavin smacked her palm with his own. "She lives in Lovett Peak."

"Are we going to Lovett Peak today?"

"Nope, no Lovett Peak for us. We're going to Texas."

"Can we swim in Texas?"

"Absolutely." Cade grabbed Gavin under the arms and lifted him in the air and jiggled him around until giggles spilled from his lips.

Jenna pinched Gavin's toes. "Shh, Beth is still sleeping."

"No, I'm not."

"Sorry."

"No problem." She executed a noisy yawn. "What time is it, anyway? I can't see the alarm clock."

Jenna peeked over Cade's body. "It's seven o'clock."

"Ooh, that's late. Even if we get out of here by eight, we won't make it to Grenfield until around eleven o'clock tonight."

Cade stopped hoisting Gavin up and down. "Grenfield?"

"It's between San Antonio and Austin. Nice, midsize town—you can blend in but not get overwhelmed."

"You're the expert. Why wasn't Grenfield your number one pick over the place in Oregon?"

"The Oregon town was on the coast. I thought you might like that better."

Jenna slipped out of bed. "How are you feeling, Beth?"

"Much better." She touched her bandage. "I think I can get rid of this today."

"Unless you need stitches." Jenna folded her arms over

her cotton nightshirt, the awkwardness of their situation highlighted by the morning sun. "Cade, let's get ready and head down to the hotel restaurant for breakfast and give Beth some privacy."

He tossed Gavin onto the bed. "It'll take me two minutes to shower."

"And Gavin had a bath after his swim last night. It won't take me more than ten minutes to shower and dress."

"Then I'll catch a few more winks of sleep." Beth buried her face in her pillow and pulled the covers over her head.

Jenna busied herself with dressing Gavin and packing up their things—again. When Cade stepped out of the bathroom, she handed Gavin over to him. "Why don't you go downstairs and get us a table. I'll join you in ten minutes."

Jenna zipped through her shower and pulled on a pair of jeans and a black turtleneck. She ran wet fingers through her dry hair to fluff it up, and then peered out of the bathroom door.

A muffled sob came from the depths of the covers on Beth's bed. Jenna crossed the room and patted her shoulder. "I'm sorry about Jeff."

Beth yanked the covers off her head, and her eyes glowed with anger. "He's going to pay—whoever was responsible."

"I'm sure he or they will once Prospero finds out who ambushed you."

"Prospero…Cade has a lot more faith in the organization than I do. He's in the field and is removed from the petty politics. It's like any other government agency, and just like any other government agency, it has its bad eggs, its slackers, its power hungry, its traitors."

"Then I guess you just have to put your faith in the men and women in the field. They'll get justice for Jeff."

"You have a lot of faith in Cade, don't you?" Beth had

scrunched up the pillow behind her back and scooted to a sitting position.

"Of course I do. He has saved me and Gavin again and again these past few days."

"That's good. You're lucky you found someone like that."

Her eyes misted over again, and Jenna patted her hand. "Prospero Team Three will avenge Jeff's death."

Jenna left Beth so she could get ready on her own, and she joined Cade and Gavin at breakfast, already digging into their food.

Cade held up his fork. "Hope you don't mind we started without you. I was expecting you sooner."

"I had a conversation with Beth. She's torn up over Jeff and doesn't seem to have a lot of confidence in Prospero to find his killers."

"We'll get the job done. We always do." He shoved his half-eaten eggs toward her. "Breakfast?"

"I'll just have some coffee. Looks like we're in for another day of sitting in the car."

By the time Beth joined them, her anger and bitterness seemed to have dissipated...along with her bandage.

Jenna asked, "Is your head okay?"

"It's fine." Beth pulled out a chair across from Cade and fluffed her hair. "I washed the, um—" she glanced at Gavin clicking two spoons together "—sticky stuff out and combed my hair over the whole mess. I'm good."

Gavin turned to Beth and put the two spoons over his eyes.

"Gavin." Jenna snatched the spoons from his hands. "Someone might want to use those spoons. Say hello to Beth. Beth, this is Gavin."

"Nice to meet you, Gavin." Beth extended her hand, and Gavin stared at it.

"She's trying to shake hands with you, silly."

Gavin put his hand in Beth's and shook it up and down about ten times.

Beth extricated her newly sticky fingers and wiped them on a napkin. "Good job."

Cade laughed. "The hazards of shaking hands with a three-year-old."

Beth ordered just a coffee like Jenna, dumped some skim milk in it and gulped half the cup. "I think we'd better get going."

"I don't think we're going to find a hotel at eleven o'clock at night, anyway." He pulled out a wad of cash. "Maybe we should stop at a halfway point."

"We don't need to find a hotel." She pointed to the cash. "I have more of that for you, too."

"Why don't we need a hotel? I'm not sleeping in that car." He winked at Jenna. "We tried that once and it didn't work out too well."

"I have keys to a place in Grenfield."

"Really?" Jenna's voice squeaked. Beth had it all planned out.

"That's how I operate. I narrow down the selections to four or five choices, and then rent a few places for a few months."

"Didn't you just get the order to resettle us a few days ago?"

Beth clicked her tongue. "How little you covert ops guys know about how we operate. We're always working on re-settlement locations—and the safe houses. These things happen on the spur of the moment. You can't expect us to come up with places within a few days."

"I'm impressed." Cade waved the check at the waitress. "So you already had some locations lined up."

"Exactly, so no hotels for us tonight. We have a little

house rented and ready to go. Oh—" a blush stole over her cheeks "—I hope you don't mind if I crash with you one more night. I'll be on my way the following day."

"Of course not. Where would you stay at eleven o'clock at night?"

Cade grabbed a napkin and wiped the syrup off Gavin's hands. "We keep talking about eleven o'clock, but if we don't get moving that's going to be eleven o'clock a.m."

He gave up on Gavin's hands and hauled him to the bathroom to wash with soap and water.

Beth tilted her chin toward them—father and son. "Looks like he's taken to parenting."

"I had no doubt about it." Actually, she'd had lots of doubts after what he'd gone through with Kevin, but with every minute Cade spent with Gavin, his confidence as a father grew.

She just hoped their stint in Grenfield, Texas, wouldn't make Cade long for bachelor life again.

On the fifteen-hour drive to Texas, the three of them switched off driving duties, took turns entertaining Gavin and even caught a nap or two.

The little car, which had seen Cade and Jenna through five states in fewer than five days, rolled onto the dark streets of Grenfield.

Beth punched up the directions on her smartphone and called out the turns to Cade in the driver's seat. When he turned on a street lit with old-fashioned streetlights, she said, "It's on the left—five eighty-two."

"This looks nice." Jenna rolled down the window. "Not too cold, either."

"Texas is known for its extremes in temperatures. Eighty degrees one day and forty-eight the next." He peered out the window and pulled up to the curb in front of a light-colored house with a big tree in the front. "I think this is five eighty-two."

He cut the engine and sat for several moments with his hands on the steering wheel.

Was he regretting this already?

"Well, let's take a look at our new—temporary—home." Jenna reached for her door handle first in the backseat.

It seemed to drag Cade out of the spell the house had seemed to cast over him. "I'll get Gavin. He'll be ready to burn some energy tomorrow."

"Just hope he stays asleep tonight or we'll never get him down."

Beth magically produced the key to the house and stepped inside first, flicking on the nearest light switch.

Homey. The furnished living room exuded an air of normalcy. This could be any room in any house in any city in America. She and Cade and Gavin would blend in. Nothing dangerous here. Nothing out of the ordinary.

"Is it okay?" Beth nibbled on her fingernail, and Jenna realized how hard her job had to be and how seriously she took it.

"It's perfect. Cade?" She turned to Cade disappearing down a short hallway with Gavin in his arms.

"Shh."

Jenna took a turn around the room and punched a button on the wall to turn on some recessed lights in the kitchen.

Cade returned to the living room, brushing his hands together. "The kid didn't make a peep."

"H-how's the house?" Beth had edged to the window and peeked through the blinds.

"It's fine. Thanks, Beth. You're a miracle worker." He jerked his thumb over his shoulder at the hallway. "And there are three bedrooms back there, so you can have your own room tonight."

"That's good, not that I don't like you guys."

"And you even have a toothbrush. I could give you a change of clothes for tomorrow. I know how hard it is running around the country in the same outfit with nothing to change into."

Beth cocked her head. "Thanks for the offer, but I'm a little bigger than you. I'll be heading back to my hotel in Arizona tomorrow, anyway."

Cade sidled next to Jenna and slipped an arm around her waist. "We still need to figure out the transportation, unless you have a car for us here, too."

"No such luck, but I can take a bus back."

"Or you can take our car, or rather Prospero's car, and we can find something else while we're here."

"You shouldn't be without transportation, Cade."

He yawned. "We'll figure it out tomorrow. You don't have to leave first thing in the morning. Rest, give us some tips for surviving with our new IDs and we'll work out the car situation."

They claimed their bedrooms, and Cade shut the door and stood with his back against it. "Ah, alone at last."

Jenna plucked a pillow from the bed and threw it at him. "That's not very nice after everything Beth did for us."

"I think she owed us after we got her out of that warehouse. She and Jeff were sloppy."

"I still don't understand what happened or who killed Jeff."

"I don't, either, but I'm going to get to the bottom of it."

She raised one eyebrow. "And how is Mr. Yardley going to do that from Grenfield, Texas?"

"I have ways." He lunged for her, grabbing her around the waist, and she squealed.

"Shh." He kissed her mouth to keep her quiet.

And it worked.

When his hands worked their way beneath her clothes, she grabbed the front of his sweatshirt. "Do you really think we should?"

"Are you kidding? Our son is finally in another bed in another room, and Beth, our constant companion for the past twenty-four hours, is in another room. I'm not wasting another minute."

He walked her backward to the bed and they fell across the mattress.

She couldn't think of one more objection. With Cade smothering her with kisses, she could barely breathe.

THE FOLLOWING MORNING, they made their first strides toward settling in by going grocery shopping, getting the gas turned on and finding the nearest park.

Cade had insisted that Beth take another day to rest before making her way back to Arizona and facing her bosses at Prospero. And she needed it.

Beth's pale face made the dark circles beneath her eyes stand out even more, and Jenna wondered if she was completely healed from her attack.

As they sat at the kitchen table eating sandwiches, Jenna poured Beth another glass of water. "I think you should see a doctor when you get back. You need to get checked out."

"You're probably right. I can see one of the doctors Prospero has on retainer—no questions asked."

"That's the way we like it."

Cade's cell phone buzzed and he checked the display. "I can't believe it. It's J.D."

He answered the phone and nodded to Jenna. "Did you make it back okay?"

He paused and replied. "Man, you have no idea."

Then he held up his finger and wandered into the back of the house.

Jenna shrugged. "Hush, hush. I'm glad J.D.'s back in the States. Maybe he can help Cade figure out some of the recent events."

"I'm glad he's back, too. I contacted him earlier to let him know Cade's new location. I figured if there was anyone I could trust, it would be J.D."

"I didn't realize you knew all of Prospero Team Three so well."

"I started around the same time they did. I was assigned to support them at first."

Cade returned to the room. "J.D.'s flying into San Antonio tonight. I'm going to pick him up at the airport."

"You're not bringing him back here." Beth crossed her arms, not a hint of humor in her face.

"Excuse me?"

Beth spread her arms. "This is a resettlement house. You're not Cade Stark here and you wouldn't know J.D. the spy. It's a rule, Cade. You can't bring him here."

"Well, he hadn't planned to stay here, anyway. We just need to talk."

"Talk at the airport." Jenna wiped Gavin's mouth and offered him an apple slice.

"I don't want to drag you and Gavin to the airport."

Beth held up her finger. "That would break another rule. Jenna and Gavin shouldn't be anywhere near J.D. You could compromise this whole location."

"I don't like leaving you. Where will you three be?"

"Right here. Where we'll be safe." Beth spread her arms. "Nothing unusual about a sister helping her sister and nephew get settled in their new home."

Jenna hid a smile beneath her hand. Beth had insisted on this charade of sisters when they looked nothing alike.

She said, "Beth's right. We'll stay here while you meet up with J.D. at the airport."

"I'm leaving a gun here. Beth, you don't carry one, do you?"

"No. If I had, Jeff might still be alive."

Cade quickly changed the subject. "Okay, then. I'll go to the airport to meet J.D., and pump him for information. Maybe he knows more about what happened to Jim back at the outpost. Maybe he knows something about what went down at the warehouse."

Beth pointed a finger at him. "And if you're made at the airport, you don't come back here."

He saluted. "Got it, Chief."

A few hours later, Cade left a gun on a shelf in the cupboard. "Just in case."

"We'll be fine." Jenna curled her arms around his neck and kissed him. "Be careful out there."

When Cade left, Jenna sank into the couch and aimed the remote at the TV. She surfed through several channels. "If we're going to stay here, we need cable in the worst way."

Beth came out of the kitchen carrying two glasses of red wine. "This will make anything on TV a little better."

Jenna took a glass from her and clinked its rim with Beth's. "So true."

Halfway through the show they were watching, Jenna put Gavin to bed. She almost curled up next to him. Everything that had happened to her since the moment she scrambled beneath the floorboards in Lovett Peak hit her at once.

She dropped onto the couch and drained her wineglass.

"Do you want another?" Beth half rose from her seat.

"No." The word felt thick on Jenna's tongue. She curled her legs beneath her, and her head drooped to the side.

"Good. Because now I'm going to take your son."

Chapter Sixteen

"It makes no sense." Cade drained his bottle of beer and started picking at the label on the wet glass.

"I don't know why you've been so paranoid about Prospero. Jack Coburn runs a tight ship. Everything over the past few days has been according to protocol. As far as I know, internal affairs dealt with Horace Jimerson." J.D. checked his watch. "And we won't be privy to his punishment for a while."

Cade picked the sticky label from his fingernails. "What about the situation at the warehouse?"

"That, I can't tell you. Why is Beth so sure Zendaris didn't ambush her and Curson? She didn't even see her attackers."

"It's not just Beth. If Zendaris's guys hit that warehouse and killed Curson, why didn't they wait for me and Jenna? They had to know we were going to show up. They've been chasing us all across the Southwest. Why give up an opportunity to snatch Gavin and hold him until I cough up the plans?"

"That whole setup seems screwy to me." J.D. kicked a boot up onto the chair across from him and crossed his arms behind his head. "You didn't see any attackers. Why didn't they kill Beth, too? Curson dies and Beth gets a bump on the head?"

"You're not suggesting Beth is working with Zendaris, like Jim, are you?"

"No, but maybe she screwed something up." J.D. tipped his chair back. "That woman has a lot of issues."

"She does?"

"She had a major crush on you for one thing."

"No way." Cade tracked back through his memories of Beth in the office, at the get-togethers and most recently on the drive to Texas. "No way."

J.D. snorted. "Man, you're so hung up on Jenna you wouldn't notice if another woman stood in front of you doing the shimmy shake."

Heat blasted Cade's face. "Yeah, I think I would."

"Really? 'Cuz those two lovely ladies in the corner have been eyeing us for a good half hour, and I swear you couldn't tell me right now if they're blondes, redheads or brunettes."

Cade slid a gaze to two women giggling over a couple of margaritas.

"Without looking." J.D. shook his head.

"So the fact that Beth had a crush on me means she has issues?"

"It's not just that. She's really self-conscious about those disfiguring scars on her back. It's done a number on her self-esteem."

"What are you talking about?" Cade's brows snapped together. "Beth doesn't have any disfiguring scars on her back."

"You've seen her back lately?"

"She stayed in our hotel room with us the other night."

J.D. lifted one eyebrow. "Was she running around naked or something?"

"Why do you keep bringing up naked women?" Cade

kicked J.D.'s chair. "She slipped off her sweater when she got into bed. I didn't notice any scars."

J.D.'s chair snapped to the floor. "That's weird because I've seen them and it's not something she can hide. They're scars from burns."

"How did it happen?"

"I'm not sure. Some accident involving her sister when they were children." He leveled his finger at Cade. "Another thing that's weird is how you ended up in Texas for your resettlement."

"Why is that weird?"

"Was Beth so tongue-tied around you she never talked about herself? She's from Texas. I think her mother still lives here, and if I'm not mistaken, it's somewhere near San Antonio."

"Coincidence."

"Maybe, but not too smart if she wants you to keep your distance from everyone connected to Prospero. Maybe she just wants you within striking range if she ever decides to go for you."

Cade chewed the inside of his cheek. Why hadn't Beth mentioned that fact?

J.D. checked his watch again. "Hey, man, I need to catch my flight. When I see Gage down in South America, I'll see if he heard anything about the warehouse. He's more removed than we are, but that guy always seems to know everything—it's those connections in high places."

Cade shoved back his chair and shook J.D.'s hand. "Thanks for stopping on your way down. Keep me in the loop if you can."

J.D. pumped his hand and slapped his shoulder. "I'd keep an eye on Beth Warren if I were you." He cocked his head. "And ask her about those scars."

Cade tossed a couple of bills on the table. *Yeah, right.*

He was going to ask Beth Warren about the scars on her back, or lack thereof.

He dropped onto the driver's seat of the car he and Jenna had dubbed *Old Faithful,* and cranked on the engine. His phone buzzed. Had J.D. found something out already?

He lifted the phone from his pocket and stared at the display, his mouth dry. *Speak of the devil.* "Hey, Beth. Is everything okay?"

"No, no." Her voice cracked and she ended on a sob. "They've taken Jenna and Gavin."

CADE CAREENED DOWN THE highway, his jaw tight, his eyes burning. He'd left them. He'd left his family again and they'd been snatched.

Beth hadn't been able to tell him much. They'd put Gavin to bed. She and Jenna had watched TV and had a glass of wine. They both fell asleep on the couch and when Beth awoke, Jenna and Gavin were gone.

How could that happen? Nobody woke up Beth? Nobody injured her? Or would she have another bump on the head?

His tires squealed as he took one of the exits to Grenfield. He knew Beth was no agent, but how did she end up bungling every assignment?

He steadied his hands on the wheel and took a deep breath. He couldn't run in the house accusing her of anything. He knew how it felt to believe nobody trusted you.

He swung into the one-car driveway to the house, rolling over the curb. He threw the car into Park and was halfway out the door before it even stopped.

Beth met him on the porch, her hands trembling, her face blotchy with tears. "I'm so sorry, Cade. I don't know how it happened."

He ran his hands along her arms, strangely warm. "Did they hurt you?"

"N-no. I told you. I was sleeping." She pushed open the door and backed up over the threshold.

"Someone broke into the house while you were all sleeping and managed to abduct my wife and son, and you didn't hear a thing? You didn't wake up?"

Her dark eyes welled with tears. "I'm so sorry. It was the wine. We drank quite a bit and both of us passed out more than fell asleep. It was stupid, but I never dreamed they'd find us here."

"Neither did I." He circled the room, taking in the two empty wineglasses on the coffee table. One chair had been upended. He followed the hallway to Gavin's room, his fists curling as he saw the empty bed.

His gaze tracked across the windows, shut against the night air. "How did they get in?"

Beth waved her arms. "I have no idea. I haven't looked around yet."

He glanced at the half-full wine bottle on the kitchen counter and his gut knotted. His gaze tracked to a pair of shoes by the door, blades of grass sticking to the wet toes.

Cade strolled to the front door and stood with his back against it. Then he pulled out his weapon. "Show me your back…Beth."

Her eyes widened, glowing with some internal fire. "Your wife and son are missing and you want me to take off my clothes? Like father, like son."

Releasing the safety on his gun, he growled. "Show me your back."

She turned slowly, gripping the edge of her blouse and glancing over her left shoulder, a small smile playing over her lips. She yanked up the blouse to reveal a smooth swath of skin.

His muscles coiled and his grip tightened on his gun. "Who are you?"

"Funny." She dropped her blouse and spun around, gripping the weapon he'd left in the cupboard. "I could've sworn Beth said she never told you about her lovely scars."

"Who are you and where are my wife and son?"

"They're safe...for now." She took a step forward and extended her left hand. "I'm Abby, Abby Warren, Beth's older and stronger twin sister."

Cade clenched his jaw so his mouth wouldn't drop open. He ignored her hand, no longer trembling. "Where's Beth?"

"Dead."

"Did you..."

"Yes, I killed her. I tried before, you know, when we were twelve. I threw scalding water at her. I was aiming for her head, but it hit her back instead." She shrugged. "Then I decided it was better to keep her around and live vicariously through her."

"If you were the stronger twin, why live through your sister? Why not live your own life?"

She made a face with an exaggerated frown. "They watched me, especially my father. I could always wrap my mother around my little finger. But Dad—" she pursed her lips "—he was always after me to take my meds. You can't live your life all doped up."

Cade steadied his gun. She must be seriously mentally ill—and she had Jenna and Gavin. "You've been posing as Beth? Why?"

"Why?" She blinked her eyes. "To get you, of course. Well, you and some big bucks from that arms dealer Nico Zendaris."

"What are you talking about?" His stomach sank. He could handle Beth...Abby, but if she'd called in Zendaris or already turned Jenna and Gavin over to him, he had a bigger obstacle in front of him than some psychotic woman with a gun.

"Beth wanted you. Didn't you know that? She had a crazy, wild crush on you. She showed me your picture, slobbering all over it. So I told her to go for it, but she's weak." Abby put on a childish, whining voice. "He's married, Abby. I'm just going to have to forget all about him."

She snapped her fingers. "Why should that stop you from getting what you want? So I set out to prove her wrong."

"How exactly did you plan on *getting* me?" Cade's phone buzzed in his pocket and he pulled it out.

Abby narrowed her eyes and leveled her gun at his heart. "You can call the police or Prospero or all your buddies on Team Three, but I still have your wife and son and I can make them die on my command. If you try to respond or make a call, I'll make you die, too. Beth might be mad, but I can live with that."

Cade held up his phone and shifted his gaze to the display—a message from J.D. *Another weird factoid Beth's mom lives in Grenfield 590 Burrows watch your back.*

Cade hit the button to delete J.D.'s message and took a deep breath. Jenna and Gavin must be two doors down at Abby's mother's house. But who else was there? Zendaris's thugs?

"I'm not calling anyone, Abby. So what is your plan and what does Zendaris have to do with it?"

She giggled. "I thought you'd never ask. Beth is good with statistics, facts and figures and logic. I'm even better. I like computers, Cade. I like computers a lot."

"You hacked into my computer and stole the plans."

"Aw, it was easy." She hunched her shoulders and almost blushed. "I already had a head start because I had some of your emails to Prospero. From there it was a breeze to get into your computer and lift those plans."

"You wanted money. Why didn't you just sell them to Zendaris?"

"I wanted you and the money. Just to prove I could do it. I figured I'd let Zendaris stew a little, blame you, go after Jenna and Gavin and maybe even succeed. But you were too good for him, Cade. The idiots he hired couldn't keep up with you. So I decided to help him."

"How was that plan going to help you get to me?"

"You'd be so distraught at losing your wife and son, you'd need a shoulder to cry on, and I would've been there for you."

His laugh was a sharp bark of disbelief. "Never. Would've. Happened."

"Or—" she twirled a strand of hair around her finger "—I could be the bad guy and sell those plans to whoever I want for big bucks. I'd share it all with you. You, Beth and I."

"Beth's dead."

Her brow wrinkled. "No, I'm doing this for Beth, too. I always made things right for Beth. I taught her how to cheat on exams. I…uh…handicapped the competition in a big race she had. This horrible professor was bothering her and I got him in trouble. Beth didn't know how to go after what she wanted, so I made sure she had it. Now I'm going to make sure she has you."

Abby's loose hold on reality could only help him at this point. "You would share that money with me?"

She stopped twirling her hair and yanked some strands from her head. "Yes."

"I really wanted to hang on to those plans myself, but I just couldn't do it."

She nodded. "You see, I can do those things that you can't bring yourself to do. I'm not bothered by my conscience. I know you worry about being like your father, but you don't have to. I'll be him for you."

A chill seized the back of his neck. How did she know

so much about him? "What happened in the warehouse, Abby?"

"I shot Jeff and hit myself on the side of the head. He was going to get you and Jenna all relocated in some nice, cozy place. I couldn't allow that."

Sweat dampened his brow. How was he going to get to Jenna and Gavin? If he tried to walk out now, Abby would shoot him, and God knows what would happen to his family.

"Of course you couldn't allow that. What now? Should we go to your mother's house and tell Jenna our plans?"

Abby's jaw dropped and the gun wavered—for a second. "M-my mother doesn't live near here."

"Come on, Abby. You don't think I knew all along that your mother lived two doors down on this same street?"

"Why didn't you say something before?"

"I wanted to wait and see how this all unfolded. I didn't realize you had the plans. That changes everything."

"I'll take you there on one condition." She pointed to the floor. "Give up your weapon and slide it toward me."

Every instinct in his body screamed *no,* but he had to get to Jenna and Gavin. He had to see if they were okay.

He reengaged the safety on his gun, ducked down and slid it toward Abby's feet. Keeping her weapon trained on him, she scooped up the gun. She shoved it between the cushions of the couch.

"Now open the door slowly and don't try anything."

As he opened the door, he could feel her breathing down his neck.

"Turn to the right and keep walking. It's the house with the flower box at the window, but then you already know that."

If only J.D.'s text had come sooner. The house with the flower box would've been Cade's first stop.

Low lights seeped from beneath the drawn blinds. When they reached the porch, Abby tossed him a set of keys. "The big, gold one opens the dead bolt and the lock on the handle."

Cade shoved the key in the dead bolt and stopped. "Is there anyone else in there?"

"Not yet, but I have one of Zendaris's men on speed dial, and he'd be more than happy to collect his cargo."

Gritting his teeth, he pushed open the door. His gaze swept the dimly lit room, and a pulse throbbed in his temple. "Where are they?"

"The house isn't that big. They're in the back. Your kid's sleeping. I gave him a little something to help him along."

Cade's fingers itched to wrap around Abby's throat, but he put one foot in front of the other to get to his family.

Abby jabbed him in the back with the gun. Could he spin around and take her right now? She'd have no problem shooting him.

"It's this room."

Cade pushed open the door, and his blood percolated through his veins, hot and rash. Abby had bound and gagged Jenna and she lay diagonal across the bed. She hadn't bothered with Gavin, parking him on the floor in the corner.

His little legs were drawn to his chest and he had one arm curled beneath his head to act as a cushion from the hard floor.

Jenna's eyes widened above the gag and she choked.

"Don't get too excited, Jenna." Abby lined her back up against the wall and leveled the gun at Cade. "We're here to tie up loose ends and you're one of them."

"Has Jenna properly met you, Abby?"

"No, she wasn't in any condition to carry on a conversation after I spiked her wine." She waved the gun at Jenna. "Take her gag off."

Cade crouched by the bed and loosened the tie behind Jenna's head, cupping her face as he did so. Her eyes, as blue as the Pacific, told him everything. She trusted him with her life right now and the life of their son.

And he wouldn't let them down.

"Step away."

Blocking his action from Abby, Cade caressed Jenna's cheek before he pushed away from the bed, the gag dangling from his hand. "This is Abby, Jenna. She's Beth Warren's twin sister and has decided to take her sister's place at Prospero. She's the one who hacked into my computer and stole the anti-drone plans."

Cade allowed Abby to babble on about her plans so that Jenna could understand how truly crazy she was.

Jenna took it all in, peppering Abby with questions. Jenna was playing it just right—not panicked, not fearful, not whiny. When had that adorable rich girl he'd married turned into this strong, capable woman?

Must've been when she had to.

"So, what's the upshot, Abby?" Jenna rolled to her back, toward the edge of the bed, giving Cade a hard stare.

His pulse leaped. Could she roll off the bed toward the wall and cover Gavin with her body while he tried to take down Abby? What happened if he missed? What happened if Abby shot him?

Jenna and Gavin would be at her mercy with nothing standing between Abby and whatever evil plan she concocted next.

"The upshot—" Abby straightened her spine along with her aim "—is that I'm going to call my contact with Zendaris and tell him his hostages are waiting. Then I'm going to sell the plans to the highest bidder."

Jenna scooted closer to the edge of the bed. "What's the point of that now? When Zendaris has me and Gavin in his clutches, it's not like Cade is going to run to your arms for comfort."

"But you'll be out of the way." Abby's brow wrinkled. "Cade will need someone, and Beth will be there for him."

Cade tensed every muscle in his body. "Beth or Abby?"

"B-both of us."

Jenna whispered. "You killed Beth."

Abby's hand began to tremble for real this time. "No. I did this for Beth, and Beth is part of me. She'll never die."

As a sob wracked Abby's body and the gun wavered, Cade yelled, "Now!"

He ducked and charged at Abby. The thump from the other side of the bed told him Jenna had rolled off the mattress.

He drove his shoulder into Abby's midsection while grabbing for her gun hand.

She wailed and got off a shot. Cade smashed her body against the wall, his fingers encircling her wrist. She yelped in pain but wouldn't release the gun.

He twisted her hand so that the gun was pointing away from him. Slowly, slowly, he turned the gun toward Abby.

Her panting stopped. Her dark eyes bore into his, and then she squeezed the trigger.

Through the blood spattering his face, he watched the light die from Abby's eyes.

Jenna screamed. "Cade? Cade?"

"I'm okay. It's Abby. She's dead."

Epilogue

Cade grabbed the chains of the swing to slow it down so Gavin could jump out of it for about the hundredth time that morning. When Gavin's legs got closer to the ground, he launched himself out of the swing, flying in the air for a few seconds before landing in the sand.

Cade grinned at his son rolling over and over in the sand. *Daredevil.* Like father, like son—and this time, that was okay.

Gavin hopped to his feet and scampered toward the yellow plastic slide to join another boy heading down on his stomach.

Holding up his hands, Cade yelled, "I'm taking a break."

A woman sitting near the slide looked up from her book. "I'll keep an eye on him."

"Thanks. I'll be right over there." He pointed to a picnic table with Jenna sitting on top and J.D. straddling the bench.

He joined Jenna on the table. "I think the SEALS could adopt some training from the playground."

J.D. punched him in the leg. "Man, you need to get in shape. All that lolling around in hotel suites has made you soft."

"Ah, I think we were in that suite for maybe six hours." Jenna grabbed Cade's hand. "You owe me some pampering. I had to wear flea market clothing and makeup from the drugstore."

"There's the girl I married." He kissed the side of her head.

"You'll get lots of pampering where you're going. Wish I could get an all-expenses-paid trip to Europe." J.D. reclined on the bench and folded his hands behind his head.

"I wish we could go home." Jenna squeezed Cade's hand tighter.

"We will. I can feel it, right, J.D.? This old cowboy's going to pick up where we left off and if he doesn't nail Zendaris, Gage will."

"Damn straight." J.D. crossed one booted ankle over his knee. "We're getting close, and now that Zendaris knows Abby Warren had the plans, he's going to get sloppy in his haste to get them back."

"But what did she do with the plans?" Jenna waved at Gavin playing with his new friend. "Maybe she already sold them."

Cade shook his head. "No way. That girl was nuts—brilliant and calculating, but nuts. She didn't know what to do with the plans once she hacked into my computer."

Jenna asked, "You know for a fact she had them?"

J.D. nodded. "We know she sent the first page to Zendaris as proof. We confiscated that computer, but that's all she had on there—the first page."

"So where's the rest?"

"While you two head off on your European vacation, I'm going back to D.C., where Abby lived before she took up residence in her twin's life." J.D. hoisted up to his elbows. "I'm going to find those plans, and then Gage is going to find Zendaris."

Cade laced his fingers with Jenna's and kissed her

pursed mouth. He wanted to kiss away her worries forever. "If anyone can do this, Prospero Team Three can."

"Look, Daddy!" Gavin was dangling by one arm from the top of the slide like a monkey.

Cade knocked J.D.'s legs from the bench with a well-aimed kick. "You look too comfortable. Go do your duty as an honorary uncle."

J.D. eyed him and Jenna through half-closed lids as he hoisted himself off the bench. "I can take a hint."

While J.D. loped toward the slide, Cade turned to Jenna and cupped her face in his hands. "I can't wait to start our lives together, even if that life begins in Europe."

She cinched his wrists with her fingers and met his gaze. "That life began the moment I met you, Cade Stark. You were always the man for me."

"Even when you lost faith in me?"

"I never lost faith in you—could've strangled you for doing the right thing when you left us to keep the secret of Gavin's birth from Zendaris, but never lost faith in you."

"You'll teach me to be a good father."

Turning her head, she laid her lips against his palm. "You don't need lessons. All Gavin needs is your love and protection, and you've provided that over and over."

And then, even with his son hooting and hollering at them, Cade took his wife in his arms and kissed her long and deep.

* * * * *

Brothers in Arms: Fully Engaged continues next month.
Look for Carol Ericson's CONCEAL, PROTECT
wherever Harlequin Intrigue books are sold!

REQUEST YOUR FREE BOOKS!
2 FREE NOVELS PLUS 2 FREE GIFTS!

♦ HARLEQUIN®

INTRIGUE®

BREATHTAKING ROMANTIC SUSPENSE

YES! Please send me 2 FREE Harlequin Intrigue® novels and my 2 FREE gifts (gifts are worth about $10). After receiving them, if I don't wish to receive any more books, I can return the shipping statement marked "cancel." If I don't cancel, I will receive 6 brand-new novels every month and be billed just $4.49 per book in the U.S. or $5.24 per book in Canada. That's a savings of at least 14% off the cover price! It's quite a bargain! Shipping and handling is just 50¢ per book in the U.S. and 75¢ per book in Canada.* I understand that accepting the 2 free books and gifts places me under no obligation to buy anything. I can always return a shipment and cancel at any time. Even if I never buy another book, the two free books and gifts are mine to keep forever.

182/382 HDN FVQV

Name _____ (PLEASE PRINT) _____

Address _____ Apt. # _____

City _____ State/Prov. _____ Zip/Postal Code _____

Signature (if under 18, a parent or guardian must sign) _____

Mail to the **Harlequin® Reader Service:**
IN U.S.A.: P.O. Box 1867, Buffalo, NY 14240-1867
IN CANADA: P.O. Box 609, Fort Erie, Ontario L2A 5X3

**Are you a subscriber to Harlequin Intrigue books
and want to receive the larger-print edition?
Call 1-800-873-8635 or visit www.ReaderService.com.**

* Terms and prices subject to change without notice. Prices do not include applicable taxes. Sales tax applicable in N.Y. Canadian residents will be charged applicable taxes. Offer not valid in Quebec. This offer is limited to one order per household. Not valid for current subscribers to Harlequin Intrigue books. All orders subject to credit approval. Credit or debit balances in a customer's account(s) may be offset by any other outstanding balance owed by or to the customer. Please allow 4 to 6 weeks for delivery. Offer available while quantities last.

Your Privacy—The Harlequin® Reader Service is committed to protecting your privacy. Our Privacy Policy is available online at www.ReaderService.com or upon request from the Harlequin Reader Service.

We make a portion of our mailing list available to reputable third parties that offer products we believe may interest you. If you prefer that we not exchange your name with third parties, or if you wish to clarify or modify your communication preferences, please visit us at www.ReaderService.com/consumerschoice or write to us at Harlequin Reader Service Preference Service, P.O. Box 9062, Buffalo, NY 14269. Include your complete name and address.

HI13

When Dee Ann Justice comes to town, only
Hilde Jacobson can see her for what she really is:
a CARDWELL RANCH TRESPASSER.
Read on for a sneak peek from USA TODAY *bestselling*
author B.J. Daniels's newest addition to the
CARDWELL RANCH *series....*

Colt saw that she had a stunned look on her face. Stunned
and disappointed. It was heartbreaking.

Without a word, he took her in his arms. Hilde was trembling. He took her over to the couch, then went to her liquor
cabinet and found some bourbon. He poured her a couple
fingers worth.

"Drink this," he said.

"Aren't you afraid what I might do liquored up?" she
asked sarcastically.

"Terrified," he said, and stood over her until she'd
downed every drop. "You want to talk about it?" he asked,
taking the empty glass from her and joining her on the
couch.

She let out a laugh. "*I* hardly believe what happened.
Why would I expect anyone else to?"

"I believe you. I believe everything you've told me."

Tears welled in her brown eyes. He drew her to him and
kissed her, holding her tightly. "I'm sorry you had to go
through this alone."

She nodded and wiped hastily at the tears as she drew
back to look at him. "You're my only hope right now. We
have to find out everything we can about this woman."
And then she told him everything, from finding the shop
vandalized to what led up to her being nearly arrested.

When she finished, he said, "We shouldn't be surprised."

"Surprised? I'm still in shock. To do something like that to yourself…"

"You knew Dee was sick."

Hilde nodded. "What will she do next? That's what worries me."

Colt didn't want to say it, but that's what worried him. "Maybe Hud has the right idea. Isn't there somewhere—"

"I'm not leaving. Dee told me that I've never had to fight for anything. Well, I'm fighting now. I'm bringing her down. One way or another."

"Hilde—"

"She has to be stopped."

"I agree. But we have to be careful. She's dangerous." He felt his phone vibrate, checked it and saw that his boss had sent him a text. "Hud wants to see me ASAP." Not good. "I don't want to leave you here alone."

"I'll be fine. Dee won this round. She won't do anything for a while and I'm not going to give her another chance to use me like she did today."

He heard the courage, as well as the determination, in her voice. Hilde was strong and, no matter what Dee had told her, she *was* a fighter.

Can Hilde and Colt stop Dee's deadly plan before it's too late?

Find out what happens next in
CARDWELL RANCH TRESPASSER. *Available March 19 from Harlequin Intrigue!*

HIEXP0413BJ

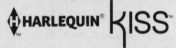